TRINITY AND
THE SHORT-TIMER

by Trevor Holliday

CONTENTS

This book is dedicated to the men and women
of the United States Army.

Also by Trevor Holliday:

Trinity Works Alone

Trinity Thinks Twice

Ferguson's Trip

THREE OF CLUBS

If the old man had fallen a few steps earlier, things would have been different.

"Snow's coming down good," Mr. Yee said.

The snow had been falling since mid afternoon.

Frank Trinity wore a dark blue turtleneck sweater like Steve McQueen in *Bullitt*.

One by one he flipped three cards into the Stetson four feet from his chair.

He didn't bother watching the snow fall.

He was occupied with the cards.

The glare of the fluorescent tubes overhead made the Quonset hut seem brighter as the afternoon wore on.

As a warrant officer in the CID, Trinity wore civilian clothing.

He bought the Stetson during his last leave in Tucson.

Despite his persistence, Trinity still fell short of mastery when tossing the cards. The most he could manage was four in a row. Inevitably, the fifth card would land on the polished lino-

leum floor of the CID office.

"Snow's coming down really good," Mr. Yee said.

Trinity didn't want to let Mr. Yee flip the cards.

Trinity knew the interpreter would beat him.

Mr. Yee throw could throw a dart between the tines of a fork.

He would have no problem dropping all fifty-two cards into

the hat.

Blindfolded.

Face up or face down.

Mr. Yee was a permanent employee at Camp Long. He would

probably be there for years to come.

Trinity, like every other American on the camp, was starting

to get short.

Soldiers started to get short the moment they stepped off the

plane in Pusan.

With five months left in Korea, Trinity was neither a short-

timer nor a newcomer.

He was mid-tour.

Thus the card-flipping.

Trinity tried another card. The three of clubs hit the brim of the Stetson before teetering onto the floor.

Trinity swiveled his chair toward the gray desk, fanned the deck onto the glass top, stood up and looked out the window.

He stretched.

The ground was covered by at least three inches of snow. It hadn't been that deep when he sat down.

"Looks like it," Trinity said. "Doesn't show any signs of letting up, either."

Small talk about weather.

Both men stood by the window.

The demands of the job on a Friday afternoon in January were not rigorous. Trinity needed to drive through the ville later in the evening, but he would let Mr. Yee go early.

Mr. Yee lived near the camp.

Trinity liked visiting with Mr. Yee at home. Mrs. Yee was a

beautiful woman who made Trinity feel at home.

Wasn't it time to go yet?

Trinity sat down again, picked up the deck of cards and gave them a quick overhand shuffle.

"Take a look at this," Mr. Yee said.

Trinity stood up. The wind carried the snow horizontally like quills of porcupines gusting down the street in front of the office.

Snow was still accumulating on Trinity's green Impala. Only the outline of the car was visible.

Mr. Yee wasn't pointing at the snow on the car.

He pointed farther down the street toward the mess hall.

An old man, his gray beard covering the front of a dark pea coat, struggled against the blowing snow and accumulating drifts. He carried a pack on his back, the kind Trinity associated with world travelers passing through Seoul.

But Seoul was a long way from Camp Long. Far under the radar of most travelers.

The old man wasn't a bum.

Even from a distance, and despite resistance from the snowy wind, Trinity recognized a military bearing in the man's gait.

He's American, Trinity thought.

Probably former military if the gate guards let him on base.

Occasionally, old soldiers returned to Korea.

They took part in junkets touring places where they served. Trinity remembered a group traveling on a bus in the late summer, not long after his own arrival at Camp Long.

What did they expect to see?

Some of them brought their wives.

They wanted to look around and remind themselves of the place where they served long-ago.

This man didn't look like one of those old soldiers.

The change of season made a difference.

But who would spend their vacation at Camp Long in winter?

The warm-weather visitors wore the same clothes they wore off-duty during their tours.

Loud polyester sweat suits.

Satin jackets emblazoned with dragons and maps of Korea.

This man wore a pea coat and a dark knit hat.

He was old.

Really old.

Trinity watched the old man marching against the wind.

He provided the only movement on the street.

No jeeps, no groups of soldiers joking their way toward the mess hall, no ajummas heading back to the ville after their jobs at the camp.

Nothing but the old man struggling against the new snow as he made his way down the street.

Trinity turned from the window and grabbed the keys to the Impala.

At least he could give the old guy a lift.

"Hey Trinity," Mr. Yee shouted, "he's fallen down."

The fall must have taken less than a second. The old man fell in the time Trinity used to turn toward the desk.

Trinity scooped the keys from the desk, grabbed his sheep drover's jacket from the back of the chair, and shook the few cards from the bottom of the Stetson.

Mr. Yee was already outside.

The two men raced in the old man's direction.

The snow swirled around them, drifting enough to disorient Trinity. Trinity regretted the slick soles of his cowboy boots. They ran toward the spot in the street where the man fell.

The snow, even deeper now, covered the spot.

The man was not there.

Trinity turned toward Yee, who stood slapping black-leather gloved hands together.

"Mess hall?"

The only building nearby wouldn't open for at least half an hour.

Sgt. Deavers opened the door of the mess hall for the two men. He watched Trinity and Mr. Yee stamp snow from their boots.

"Didn't see nobody," Deavers said.

He was a large man. The temperature was high in the mess hall. Deavers only wore an olive t-shirt above his fatigue pants.

Two KATUSA soldiers came up to the door.

"Not time yet, fellows," Deavers said to the Koreans.

He looked toward Trinity and Mr. Yee.

"See what you've done?"

"Thanks," Trinity said.

"I didn't see anybody out there," Deavers said. "Can't say I was looking, though."

Trinity and Yee walked back to the Quonset hut. The snow was falling at an incredible rate. Snow covered both men's boots.

They didn't discuss the old man.

He had gotten up and gone somewhere.

What was so unusual about seeing this old man?

Trinity looked out the window.

The approaching evening darkness took over the sky.

The streetlights of Camp Long came on.

THE BUS

Harmony Ecklund could barely see the bus driver.

In the dark, only the glow of his cigarette made him visible.

Chad is a nightmare, Harmony thought.

The bus felt somber now, pushing steadily through the dark Korean night.

She thought about her students. Three of them had gone to the bus terminal to see her off.

Her students liked her.

Loved her, maybe.

She looked at Chad, quietly sleeping off his fury.

Rage, fueled by booze, kept him screaming at her for the first part of the trip.

All the way to Seoul, right before they changed buses. Now Chad was sleeping through one of the worst snowstorms Harmony had ever seen.

He started his attack as soon as they got on the bus. Even the poor little girls in their black and white school uniforms who came to see Harmony off were fair game for Chad's venom.

She never should have left the school with him.

She should have talked to the principal one more time.

She looked at Chad's body slumped into the seat of the almost completely empty bus.

The snow didn't look like it would stop.

It was now dark outside and they were headed into a remote part of the country.

Nightmare isn't the right word, she thought.

She needed to do something.

He's worse than a nightmare.

She wished she had never met him.

She wished she hadn't been taken in by his now transparent charm.

Her motives were good.

She wanted adventure.

She thought teaching English in Korea would be an adventure.

It would have been one, too.

It *was* an adventure at first.

Before she allowed herself to be taken in by Chad.

She looked at his face. His carefully styled moustache and his mass of disheveled hair.

A poet.

Who the hell cares?

His writing didn't impress her. Of course to Chad, her lack of fawning appreciation of his poems only meant she was unsophisticated.

He wrote *haiku*.

She could suggest a title for his first collection:

SMALL POEMS FROM A SMALL PERSON.

She hated herself for following him.

She hated herself for getting on the bus.

She hated herself for being with him now.

Right now, she thought, heading God only knows where.

The new school was Chad's discovery.

A great new school which promised to pay the two of them so much more than they were earning now.

This wonderful, incredible school would treat them with so much more *deference*.

Bastard, she thought.

Their school had treated *her* with more than enough deference.

Chad was snoring.

Exhaling makkoli, the cheap rice wine he used to fuel his tirades.

Bastard.

Chad thought the new school would recognize his greatness.

He actually *used* those words.

Chad, being so great a man, didn't merely go to Mr. Lee to turn in his own resignation.

No, Chad told Mr. Lee neither he nor Harmony could teach there any longer.

And Mr. Lee accepted their joint resignation.

Harmony tried to explain, but Mr. Lee just looked sad and held up his hands in an uncomprehending gesture.

She no longer had her job.

Harmony's mistake compounded with each mile of this snowy journey into nowhere.

Two hours since Seoul.

She needed to *do* something.

Where were they?

Even in daylight, before the snow started to fall, Harmony didn't know where they were. The signs indicated exits to towns she'd never heard of.

Did she think to bring a map?

She got out of her seat and steadied herself on the cushioned top of the empty seat in front of her. Using the seats for stability she stumbled toward the front of the bus.

"What is the next town?"

The driver didn't turn. He held the cigarette between two fingers of his right hand.

"Town?"

A translation problem, she thought. She tried to re-phrase her question.

The driver shook his head and pointed toward the windshield with the cigarette. Harmony saw a few dim lights ahead.

He shook his head again.

It wasn't much of a town.

The snow made visibility nearly impossible. She didn't want to distract the driver.

She walked back to her seat.

Thank God, she thought.

At least her luggage wouldn't cause a problem.

She only carried a backpack.

Nothing under the bus.

Unfortunately, her backpack was wedged next to Chad's. It perched in the bin directly over his head. She would have to pull her own pack free without dislodging Chad's.

She couldn't risk Chad's backpack falling. She couldn't catch it.

It weighed a ton.

And she couldn't risk waking him.

She made her way precariously back to the driver.

"How far to the town?" she asked. She hoped she was asking the question in a polite fashion.

"Soon."

Harmony put her hand on his arm.

"I need to get off the bus here."

She pointed back at Chad.

"That man stays on the bus. He's crazy. Meechu-so."

The bus driver didn't answer, but he couldn't have helped hearing Chad.

Chad had been loud.

The town was not promising. The few lights and the snow made it look yellow.

The bus pulled to the side of the road. The driver opened the door.

Harmony held her breath and tugged at the backpack.

It came free. She took one last look at Chad. Would she miss him? She wasn't sure. She knew she needed to get away from him.

The flapping canvas in front of the bus obscured a man roasting chestnuts over a blue flame. She got off the over-heated bus and felt the cold snowy air around her.

The chestnut vendor stared at her.

She was used to stares. She was taller than most Korean men, and her blonde hair, even under a knit cap, attracted attention.

Some of her students said she looked like a movie star.

Well, this is one role she never expected to play.

She was on the street in a blizzard.

It was dark and cold as hell.

Harmony's grasp of Korean was limited.

Her money was limited.

She blew a kiss toward the bus as it drove away.

The bus would take Chad away and out of her life.

Without Chad she could start to live her own life again.

And wasn't this what she wanted?

Wasn't this why she came to Korea in the first place? Hadn't she wanted an adventure?

Well, she was having one now.

She looked around. The streets were deserted, though she saw light through some windows.

What was she going to do? Would she start knocking on doors asking for shelter?

She needed to find a yogwan. A little traveler's inn.

She could forget trying to read signs.

Harmony's Korean was strictly verbal.

Harmony ducked under the canvas flap, smelling the rich aroma of the hot chestnuts.

The vendor twisted a cone of paper and shoveled in a scoop.

She dug into her wallet and pulled out some won.

"Kamsahamnida," she said.

The vendor smiled and nodded.

She was hungry, and the chestnuts would help.

She put her pack on her back.

It wasn't too heavy.

She could manage the weight.

She started to walk.

FROZEN CHOSUN

How far did he walk today?

The old man didn't know. He started the morning in the little yogwan he found the previous night.

A perfectly adequate place run by a decent man.

Awakening, he heard the sounds of the Korean town coming to life.

Bottles clattering in the alley.

A rooster crowing.

A woman yelling.

Who could say about what?

The old man's Korean never was very good.

It was better after all these years, but the woman's yelling was too fast and too incoherent for him to understand more than a few words.

He drifted in and out of sleep the first few minutes of the day, warm under the heavy quilted blanket.

The charcoal stove in the center of the room heated the yellow linoleum floor, but it could also be a death trap.

He remembered checking the stovepipe before going to sleep and cracking open the small window above his head. The smoke was supposed to rise through the flimsy stovepipe, but the old man always took extra precautions.

The small room was the innkeeper's last available.

He looked at the stove again.

Carbon monoxide did not always behave predictably. Death would come if the charcoal burned without proper venting.

It happened frequently.

But it wouldn't happen to him.

Death wouldn't cheat him.

He was comfortable in the warmth of the room until he re-membered why he was here.

This was not a pleasure trip.

After leaving the yogwan, he spent the day walking.

The weather was cold, but the snow only recently started.

He could feel where he fell by the mess hall.

It would become a bruise.

Nothing broken.

He pushed forward into the snow.

In decent weather he could walk around the base in an hour.

How many times had he walked the camp's perimeter? How many times did he look over the bridge into the river? In summer the river beneath the bridge fed the rice and made the soil rich. It was a wide, turbulent river.

In winter, ice covered the river.

The snow still came down, covering the ice. He couldn't remember seeing it this bad.

Not since the war, anyway.

Frozen Chosun, they called Korea during the war.

Back then, all the trees were burned for fuel.

How many years ago?

It felt like a century.

The fall by the mess hall wasn't serious. He would be fine.

In most respects, he was in good shape.

In good shape for an old man.

When did he start thinking of himself that way?

He wasn't old.

Compared to old men he knew who spent their last years in front of a television?

He wasn't old at all.

Snow broke the impact of his fall.

He barely felt it happen.

He was a combat veteran, after all.

He covered his tracks from habit and left no trace of the fall.

He dusted the snow from his coat and pushed on against the wind and the snow, heading out the gates of the camp and back toward the town.

He felt himself again.

No broken bones.

He was fine.

He didn't need to go around the camp one more time. Truthfully, he couldn't face looking down from the bridge again.

The row of Quonset huts stopped after the mess hall where a line of newer barracks started.

He passed the motor pool gates. The descending road was terraced for rice paddies. The road would take him through the gates of Camp Long and onto the dirt road outskirts of the town.

The road led to the town center, and eventually back to the charcoal-heated room in the yogwan.

Back to another night of a sleep.

He knew Camp Long well.

This wasn't his first trip.

A jeep passed him.

The KATUSA driver used chains on the vehicle. The chains weren't necessary. An officer sat in the back of the jeep.

The old man shook his head.

He didn't approve of the officer sitting in the back seat.

A Korean officer would probably ride in the back, but it was overly formal for an American officer.

The KATUSA ground the gears of the jeep while shifting. The young Koreans attached to the American forces were seldom experienced drivers. The old man remembered teaching some of the men. Most of them didn't know how to drive before their enlistment and many wouldn't drive after. But as KATUSA soldiers, they were generally assigned as chauffeurs to American officers.

The KATUSA soldier got the jeep into gear and the vehicle lurched forward.

The old man continued to walk.

The soldier who stepped in front of him could have been a ghost.

The old man stopped and pushed the snow from his eyes with his gloved hands.

The nametag stitched on the soldier's field jacket read GEN-TLE.

The soldier was young.

He looked like his son.

The old man tried to think how old his own son would be, but found thinking about dates and years confusing.

How many years since his own son disappeared?

It happened such a long time ago, details were confused.

The MP on duty at the gate barely poked his head out from the guard shack to acknowledge the old man leaving the post.

The road into the town was bad and the snow made it worse. The old man thought about catching a taxi.

It's not that bad, he thought.

He would walk the last mile slowly.

He would be back at the yogwan before long.

He thought about the charcoal fire. It would be warm inside his room.

He would check the stovepipe, crack the window, and fall asleep again.

The snow swirling under the street lights showed no signs of stopping.

CORCORANS
AND KOOLS

Spec 4 Ben Gentle practiced his kata.

He worked through the mechanics of the movements slowly and precisely.

Standing in front of his closed wall locker, stripped to his T-shirt, Gentle clenched his fists the way Mr. Yee taught him, concentrating on the breath entering and leaving his body.

He thrust his right fist toward the metal locker, feeling the force of his whole body, a compact version of the entire universe, drawing to a single point.

His fist stopped just short of the locker.

The width of a dime separated his extended knuckle from the locker door.

He heard clapping.

"Too much, Bruce Lee. Take a break."

Kilkenny, Gentle thought.

He dropped his fist.

SSG Kilkenny didn't live in the Texas barracks.

Nobody over the rank of Spec 4 did, but Kilkenny spent enough time there. Kilkenny came in occasionally on the pretense of a walk-through inspection and then would stay, pulling an OB beer from the fridge. Maybe telling a war story.

For a lifer, Kilkenny wasn't half-bad.

Some night he picked this time.

Pitch black and snowing like a son-of-a-bitch outside, Gentle had almost leveled a civilian outside the barracks.

What the hell was the old man doing out there?

Snow still dusted Gentle's Corcoran boots and his field jacket, even though the furnace in the Quonset hut was going full blast.

Gentle almost felt hot.

He felt self-conscious with Kilkenny here. He pulled a pack of Kools from the pocket of the fatigue shirt he had tossed on his bunk and lighted one from the pack of AFEES matches he kept under the cigarette pack's cellophane wrapper.

Kilkenny stood next to the refrigerator. Opened it and took one of the OBs. Gentle didn't give a shit if Kilkenny took the whole case.

They weren't his beers.

Probably they belonged to Sutherland.

Sutherland would drink anything.

Gentle only drank OBs when he was in the ville.

Gentle was in a good mood.

He was short.

A single-digit midget.

"Going out, Gentle?"

SSGT Kilkenny held the bottle loosely.

He was a tall, raw-boned Pennsylvanian and he liked to talk.

For a lifer, he's not a bad guy, Gentle thought.

Kilkenny opened the bottle.

"Shit no," Gentle said, "I'm too short."

He took a drag on the Kool.

Thought about it.

"Maybe for a half hour."

There was nothing in the ville Gentle wanted to see. Watch newbie's getting drunk and trying to muster their courage with the Mustang Club girls?

He'd seen enough.

All Spec 4 Ben Gentle wanted to do was to go home.

He looked at Kilkenny.

"You going?"

Kilkenny shook his head.

"I'm on the wagon," Kilkenny said.

He brought the OB to his lips.

Laughed.

"As far as anyone knows."

Gentle shook his head.

"That shit's not beer anyway."

"When's your plane leave?"

Gentle looked at his reflection in the locker mirror. How long would it take to readjust to the world?

Kilkenny took another drink.

Looked at Gentle.

"Just a reminder," he said. "Major Friend is a major asshole."

What else is new? Gentle thought.

Friend hadn't made a good start and he'd gotten worse.

"In what sense?" Gentle said.

Kilkenny frowned.

"In every fucking sense," he said. "He's had a hard-on about something for days."

Like I care, Gentle thought.

"Just don't give him a chance to mess with you," Kilkenny said. "He's got some new rules. No overnights your last week. You got what, four days? You're probably better off laying low."

Kilkenny was right, and Gentle knew it.

If Gentle stayed out after curfew this week, Friend would bust him.

Everyone knew Friend's rule was horseshit. In the past, fifteen minutes past curfew, even a half hour was no sweat.

That was *then*, and it didn't matter.

This was *now*.

Major Friend made it clear.

No more curfew violations... Nobody in the off limits area...

Particularly not short-timers.

Offenders would be *lucky* to leave country without any stripes.

Friend meant it too.

Like Kilkenny said, Major Friend was a major asshole.

Gentle held his hand out, palm-side down.

Looked straight at Kilkenny.

"That's me, baby," he said, "flying under the fucking radar."

* * *

Gentle lasted twenty minutes in the barracks after Kilkenny left.

How much trouble could he get into, after all?

He was four days short.

He would head home in four days.

He was so short he could play handball on a fucking curb.

Three days and a duffel bag drag.

The barracks were empty.

Gentle decided to go down to the ville.

Catcher in the Rye, he thought.

He'd read a lot of books during his tour.

At least *that* was constructive, he thought.

And he'd studied with Mr. Yee in the dojang near the gates, repeating the dance-like movements of each kata until Mr. Yee was satisfied.

Like Holden Caulfield, he thought, walking around Pencey Prep after he's gotten the boot.

Just walking around to see if there's something he'll miss.

Gentle looked at the mirror.

He needed a deerstalker hat.

✻ ✻ ✻

He wore civilian clothes.

Jeans, flannel shirt, leather jacket.

Cold as hell outside and snow still coming down.

Walking through the gate, the guards barely noticed him.

❊ ❊ ❊

Gentle sat in a back booth at the Mustang Club and ordered an OB from the waitress.

Bedraggled Christmas ornaments still hung over the bar.

A cut-out Santa rode a sled along the wall, and a string of lights winked from under the bar.

The girl was cute. Gentle hadn't seen her before.

She wore a white plastic nametag.

MUSTANG CLUB

SUNNY # 5

"You're number five?" Gentle said.

Sunny giggled.

Gentle made a face.

"You should be in pictures."

He wondered what it would be like at home.

Christmas and New Years were over.

He'd missed all that.

He'd missed a lot.

What would he do when he got back home?

He'd thought about re-enlistment. There was something to be said for the idea.

Not much, but something.

Wouldn't it be something to re-up his last day in-country?

Fuck that shit.

How many years did Kilkenny have in?

Too long to be an E-6, Gentle thought.

Gentle drummed his fingers against the table, remembering one of the marching songs from basic:

...Re-up, re-up you're crazy -

Re-up, re-up you've lost your mind...

All he wanted to do was go home. He regretted coming coming down here.

Three days short, a huge snowstorm, and he's sitting by himself in the ville.

What kind of shit was this?

He looked around the bar.

Would he miss any of this?

He wondered.

Probably not.

He'd spent too much of his year in this spot. What was there to see?

Fighting, drinking, discontent.

Old news.

The time got away from him.

He didn't feel drunk, but he didn't feel sober, either.

The Mustang Club was nearly empty.

A fat lifer sat at the bar talking to the lady bartender. In the glass corner cubicle the blind DJ played Skynard.

It wasn't nearly last call.

The DJ hadn't played *Stateside.*

Gentle loved that song.

Everybody did. Not just the lifers.

Mel Tillis was singing about Tokyo in *Stateside,* otherwise everything was same-same.

Gentle liked the DJ.

He sometimes gave the guy cigarettes.

Sunny # Five had left.

Gentle didn't care.

He was too short.

Holden Caulfield, Gentle thought.

I'm looking for someone to say goodbye to.

The fat lifer had left.

With Sunny # 5?

How long had he been here?

Longer than twenty minutes.

A hell of a lot longer.

Things got very vague.

BEFORE CURFEW

I could freeze to death out here.

I'd be just like the little match girl, Harmony thought.

She stood on the street, her backpack beside her. She knew she had a throwaway lighter in the pack somewhere. She was dying for a cigarette.

The first place she tried to get a room was a disaster. She wondered if it was even a yogwan at all.

The man with the dark moustache rushing out of the yogwan while she knocked on the door had to be Army.

His moustache made her think of Chad.

Harmony tried to ask him if the place rented rooms, but he pretended not to hear her.

He saw her, though.

Just like Chad, she thought.

He'd looked her over before getting into the back seat of a

jeep.

He'd pulled his green knit scarf tightly, gotten into the jeep, and said something to the driver.

The gears of the vehicle ground pulling away.

I could have hitched a ride with him, she thought.

And ended up with another Chad.

The woman who came to the door was unfriendly. She didn't respond to Harmony's Korean.

"Do you have a room?"

The woman shook her head.

"No room," she said.

Same at the place next door.

The man at the door wore a V-neck and rubber sandals.

He pointed toward the street.

Harmony pulled her jacket closer to her body.

She could freeze to death out here, and who would know?

Eventually, everyone.

Her family, her friends.

Chad.

She turned away from the yogwan.

It was warm inside. She felt a wave of heat from where she stood by the door.

She would have loved to at least spend a few minutes there.

The stores were closed. She pulled up the sleeve of her jacket and felt the snow as she glanced at her watch.

Eventually it would be curfew. She would be on the street, freezing.

She remembered the survival unit she had taken in a high school biology class. A person needed water, food, and shelter to survive.

She could start screaming.

Would anyone even hear me?

The snow was now so thick it would muffle any noise she made.

❋ ❋ ❋

"What are you doing out here?"

The voice came from behind her.

She turned around.

The man was old.

His beard and his black knit cap were flecked with snowflakes.

He looked kindly. The expression of concern on his face made her feel like crying. She felt as if she was six years old.

"I can't find a place," she said.

"You're not from the base?"

The man coughed. A deep hacking cough. He sounded sick.

Harmony shook her head.

She would have to struggle not to cry.

"There's a place across the street," he said, pointing at the first yogwan she had tried.

"Follow me... They'll have room for you."

❉ ❉ ❉

He must have been my guardian angel, she thought.

It was the same place where she had seen the man with the moustache rush out.

At first, the woman at the yogwan didn't want to let her in.

She yelled something.

Too quickly.

Harmony didn't have the slightest chance of understanding her.

She crossed his arms and blocked her path.

The old man said something to the innkeeper then turned to Harmony.

"Come on," he said. "Take off your shoes. This lady here is going to let you have my room. She has another place for me."

Harmony could have kissed the old man, but she didn't get a chance. By the time she took off her hiking boots and pulled the heavy gray socks from her legs the old man had left.

He said the innkeeper had another room for him.

Her little room was cozy. A furnace stood in the center of the room and the woman took a pair of tongs and dropped a briquette on top of the one already burning.

It was more than warm now.

It felt good getting out of the clothes she'd worn all day.

She snuggled under the thick quilt and pulled it up under her chin.

Glanced around the little room with its sliding door and the calendar on the wall.

The window in the upper reaches of the room was slightly ajar.

She'd made sure before lying down.

She was safe and warm.

THE LETTER

The flashlight cut a bright beam through the dark of the closed office and came to rest on the letter. It lay on the glass top of the desk where he left it.

Major Stanley Friend exhaled quickly.

A close call.

Thank God the cleaning woman hadn't done anything with the letter.

Obviously she couldn't read the damn thing, but...

But she could have put it where someone else could read it.

Like the E-4 assigned to the office.

That one, he thought.

He'd had his eye on her... She looked sneaky enough to read a personal letter.

He'd gotten all the way to the ville before remembering the letter.

Strange, he thought.

Who was the woman he'd just seen?

The tall blonde one.

He'd never seen her on base.

He would have remembered her.

What was she doing in the ville?

He picked the letter up and stuffed it under his field jacket. He needed to look at it again. Read it through once more before deciding how to proceed.

He didn't need this letter.

Not now.

Not ever.

If someone read it, they woudn't understand the meaning hidden within the text.

They couldn't read between the lines, like he could.

Nevertheless, seeing the letter sent a chill through him.

It was a warning.

Do what we say.

Or else.

Right on his office desk.

He read the letter again.

He heard the woman's accent while reading it.

It took him some time to realize she was neither Korean nor American.

And when he realized exactly *what* she was, it was too late.

❊ ❊ ❊

Forgetting to take the letter with him bothered Friend.

If nothing else, Major Stan Friend was methodical. Leaving the letter behind was sloppy.

It made Friend nervous.

The snow was unbelievable. How long would it keep coming down?

The KATUSA driver sat behind the wheel of the jeep.

"Same place," Friend said.

PFC Chun started the jeep.

The roads could get nastier than this, Friend thought. He needed to make this quick. The situation could get out of hand if he let it.

But Friend didn't intend to let matters get out of hand.

The goddamn letter.

How the hell did the woman get it on his desk?

The letter could send him to prison.

His mind raced.

Was the blonde woman one of *them*?

It seemed unlikely, but who the hell knew?

Major Friend's jeep rolled through the gate.

The MP snapped to attention and saluted.

DEEP BLUE EYES

Trinity stopped in front of the noodle shop.

The lights in the shop were bright behind the plate glass.

He pushed the door open and steam from the kitchen met his cold face. He took off his hat and stamped his boots.

Mr. Yee followed him.

The old man sat in the corner with his coat off.

"Sit, sit..." the old man smacked the chair next to him.

The same man who had disappeared in the snow.

A Korean ballad played overhead. A romantic male voice, joined by an eager soprano.

Trinity listened.

Sentimental, slightly out of key.

Unremarkable.

"You scared us," Trinity said. "Mr. Yee saw you fall."

"I'm fine," the man said. "Thanks anyway. I've taken worse falls."

He coughed. Pulled out a handkerchief and honked.

He told Trinity he would be going back to his own place soon.

"A little yogwan," he said. "Around the corner."

Trinity looked out the window. The snow still flew sideways.

"We'll give you a ride, won't we Mr. Yee?"

Mr. Yee agreed.

"No need for it, I'll just finish this and go out. Don't think about it again."

What was the old man doing? This was no time for walking.

A man in an apron approached the table.

"Coffee," Trinity said. He motioned toward the bowl of noodles in front of the old man. "And some of those, too."

Mr. Yee said something to the man in Korean.

The man laughed.

The old man pulled the bowl of noodles closer and speared a cube of tofu from the steaming broth.

"What brings you here?"

Trinity leaned forward, holding his Stetson in his hands like a frontier confessor.

The man's eyes were deep and blue.

He looked directly into Trinity's eyes until Trinity turned away.

"I'm looking for my son."

Trinity tried the noodles.

The old man was looking for his son in winter?

At Camp Long?

The man's son would probably be older than Trinity. He would have to be in his forties.

"Were you going to meet your son somewhere?"

The man's expression gave nothing away.

"No," he said. "My son is missing."

Missing?

The son could even be in his fifties.

"He's stationed here? What's his name?"

"His name was Paul."

Was.

Past tense.

Missing...

The man in the apron brought Trinity the noodles.

A plume of steam rose from the bowl.

A still life.

Trinity inspected the noodles.

"Paul Henderson."

The man looked sideways at the door to the kitchen.

The man in the apron yelled something.

The old man leaned toward Trinity.

"My name is Caleb Henderson."

Henderson's expression didn't change.

A celebrated hero like Cal Henderson would be modest.

Without a trace of arrogance.

He simply introduced himself.

One soldier to another.

Caleb Henderson was legendary.

He was one of the Army's most decorated living soldiers.

Trinity remembered an article in *Stars and Stripes* about Henderson.

Trinity extended his hand.

"Frank Trinity," he said. "It's an honor."

Henderson shook Trinity's hand with a firm grip.

The "reluctant warrior" they called him.

Something like that.

Henderson was a latter-day Sergeant York.

Refused a commission offered personally by MacArthur.

Refused Hollywood's offer to turn him into a matinee idol.

Hadn't he stayed in the Army?

Trinity thought so.

Retired decades ago as a Sergeant Major.

The *Stars and Stripes* covered that, too.

Henderson wouldn't have wanted a huge whoop-de-doo.

The face Hollywood wanted in pictures was lined now.

Who did he remind Trinity of?

Randolph Scott?

Henderson wouldn't have looked out of place in the movies.

But there was also a darkness under the surface of Henderson's skin.

He's got some memories, Trinity thought.

Trinity realized Henderson reminded him of an El Greco from one of the museums he'd visited with Valerie.

El Greco's penitent St. Peter.

Strong hands and a gray beard.

A face turned heavenward, seeking forgiveness.

For a moment, Trinity thought of Valerie Girard.

How much time had passed?

Not long enough to heal the wound Trinity sustained on the rainy night in Lyon when a drunken driver killed Valerie.

Three days before their wedding.

"You're looking for your son?"

"I have been for years. I still hold out hope."

His tone did not invite further discussion.

Trinity looked at Mr. Yee.

The interpreter was lost in thought.

Trinity picked up a soup spoon and pushed at the broth.

It was too hot to eat.

"You have a place, then?"

Henderson smiled.

The face of the penitent disappeared.

"Around the corner. It's perfect for me."

The smile reassured Trinity.

Henderson had survived in battle.

He could take care of himself.

Henderson stood up, his military bearing unmistakable.

"It was a pleasure meeting you, Trinity. How long before you go stateside?"

"At least another five months. I may be extended."

Putting on his hat and coat turned Henderson into an old man.

The same old man Trinity and Mr. Yee saw walking in the snow.

Trinity turned to Mr. Yee.

"Ready?"

Mr. Yee already had put on his coat.

THREE HOTS
AND A COT

The MP's saluted Major Stanley Friend. Nothing unusual. They saw his jeep leave any hour of the day or night, even after curfew.

The snow stopped.

Friend checked his watch and turned back toward the driver.

"I'll be out in a few minutes."

PFC Chun looked straight ahead.

A stoic.

Even with his breath visible in the single digit temperature. His GI issue pile cap covered most of his face.

Well, ultimately, Friend thought, who the hell cares? The heater works. Chun couldn't complain. With his size, he was lucky not to be up on the DMZ right now, staring into the face of one of Pyongyang's finest.

Duty would be a lot tougher up there.

PFC Chun could damn well be assured of that.

So he had to put up with a little cold...

At least he got three square meals a day. American food, too. Not the nauseating stuff Friend saw the KATUSAS eating in their own snack bar.

And they billeted in American barracks, too.

Three hots and a cot.

What more could Chun ask for?

Friend approached the hootch. Fumbled through his pocket for his key.

Things could be much worse for young PFC Chun.

Things could be far worse.

* * *

"Good evening, Major Friend."

Friend looked at her.

It felt like a kick in the stomach.

Of course she had found him.

Even getting the place off post hadn't helped.

She looked the same as she had in Seoul.

Her expensive apartment and designer clothing had given her an aura of sophistication.

He didn't know how dangerous she was.

By the time he had figured out she was a spy, he was already compromised.

✳ ✳ ✳

She was the most dangerous person he'd ever met.

He knocked the snow from his boots.

They had only met by chance.

Friend avoided the company of local women, but had been flattered by her attention.

He had met her on a tour of Cheju-do.

She said she was visiting relatives.

Visiting from California.

Thus her perfect English.

But the accent…

"How much longer do you plan to stay here, Stanley?"

The question angered Friend.

He didn't answer.

She pursed her lips and squinted.

"I'm asking you," she said, "how much longer?"

"Three months. You know that."

She knew how much longer he would be here.

Just as well as he did.

She knew everything about him.

"Then what? Where are you going next?"

Friend would ignore her.

Get himself a drink.

"Then what?"

He picked up the bottle of Jim Beam from the black lacquered side table. He had bought it, of course. Part of his own Class Six liquor rations.

Part of his job was to monitor GI purchases.

Scan a monthly list of how much potential contraband was being purchased at the PX.

Jars of mayonnaise, cartons of Kent cigarettes, those always caught his attention.

It seemed so trivial now.

He kept his own purchases to a reasonable level.

One bottle of liquor every week.

A carton of cigarettes. Two cases of beer.

Nothing out of the ordinary.

Friend had always been careful. He didn't want to ruin his career.

A few gifts down in the village though, couldn't hurt.

It was almost expected.

It was his own, personal business.

He measured a shot of the Jim Beam into a glass.

Looked through the amber liquid.

It was too light.

The cleaning woman, he thought. She's watered it down.

"You're not off the hook, you know."

The woman was speaking directly at him.

Giving him orders.

"We can discuss this," he said.

He filled the tumbler.

It was definitely watered down.

Goddamn cleaning woman.

He sipped it. Sipped it again.

Placed the glass down.

"Actually," he said, "I'd much prefer discussing this under different circumstances."

Did she understand?

Friend wondered.

Was she even listening?

He considered the letter in his pocket.

He'd turned around and gone all the way back to base to grab the letter from his desk.

He could have destroyed the letter, but there would always be another one.

How in hell did he get into this situation?

Stanley Friend.

A regular guy from Detroit.

He shook his head. Sipped the bourbon.

Mostly water.

He put the tumbler down carefully then picked it back up and slammed it onto the counter.

He watched her eyes narrow.

How did she think she could get away with it?

She's not nearly as smart as she thinks.

It was not the first time he'd tried convincing himself.

Does anyone know she's here?

He thought of the blonde woman.

Shook his head. That was just crazy.

The woman said she would expose him to the authorities.

This was more than a little black market violation.

They would call it espionage.

He had told her a little this and a little that.

Nothing of substance. Nothing too highly classified, he thought.

But they wouldn't look at it that way, and he knew it.

She was a foreign agent, and he had given her information.

He could kill her.

Yes, he really could.

And really, he probably should.

He looked at her face.

She expected an answer.

He sipped the drink again.

He would talk to the cleaning woman about the Jim Beam.

"Do you think you're off the hook?"

Friend shook his head.

"Things have changed," he said. "It's over."

He filled the tumbler to the brim.

Sipped it to keep it from spilling.

It might as well *be* ice tea.

Keep giving her what she wanted and he would never be allowed to stop.

Never.

"I'm not giving you anything more," Friend said. "By the way, I think you're bluffing."

She laughed.

"Maybe they'll kill you." she said. "It's not my call."

He believed her.

But he didn't think her people would kill him.

He was an asset.

You don't kill the golden goose.

Friend drained the weak booze in a single, extended gulp.

Friend knew they wouldn't kill him.

Not in a million years.

Because they had him.

They *needed* him.

But he was finished.

Stanley Friend.

Formerly of Detroit.

Finished.

He looked at her.

He had to do something.

He held the empty tumbler in his left hand. Worked it around in his grip like Mickey Lolich

The tumbler fit his hand perfectly.

"I've called them," she said.

Friend had idolized Lolich, pot-belly and all.

A left-hander.

Just like Friend.

The glass flew from his hand.

High and tight.

He hadn't intended to throw it at all.

Too high for chin music.

It caught her squarely above the eye and she went down.

Quicker than Tony Conigliaro had gone down.

The tumbler didn't shatter.

It fell to the floor and rolled.

Friend felt an immense sickness in his stomach. He lurched toward her.

She lay on the floor with a slash of blood over her eyebrow.

He froze.

What had he done?

She lifted her head from the floor and moaned before getting up and slapping Friend twice in the face.

He felt the start of a welt.

Holding his arms over his face in a defensive posture, Friend moved toward the door.

She blocked him.

Wedging her body in front of him, face now bloody.

Friend picked up the bottle.

Enraged.

What did she mean when she said she'd called her people?

Who did she call?

There would be no end to any of it.

There would be no end until he was finally arrested.

By his own people.

Major Stanley Friend held the bottle by the neck. It felt good in his hands, like baseball bat.

He took a practice swing.

He held the empty bottle aloft, like Norm Cash in the on-deck circle.

Norm Cash.

Stormin' Norman.

The Tigers had been something.

Cash, Kaline, Lolich, McClain.

Something.

He took another step toward her.

Took another practice swing.

She wouldn't get away with it.

He wouldn't let her.

❉ ❉ ❉

The woman lay at Friend's feet.

What have I done? he thought.

Quickly, his thoughts turned to self-preservation.

He couldn't leave her here.

Not in his place.

He wouldn't allow himself to go to a Korean jail.

Not for this.

He would have to take her somewhere.

Somewhere close.

The Mustang Club.

Just a few doors away.

He'd break in if he needed to.

Checked his watch.

Past curfew.

Picked her up.

She was surprisingly light.

* * *

The door had been easy to open. The frame splintered, but accidents happened.

He placed the woman behind the bar.

Wearing leather gloves, he picked up a nametag from the bar.

MUSTANG CLUB

SUNNY # 5

Friend hesitated, then pinned the nametag to the woman's blouse.

They would find her in the morning.

FISH JERKY

Spec 4 Ben Gentle woke up on the floor under the booth with the leather jacket he'd bought in Itaewon draped over his head.

Shit, Gentle thought.

The lifers were gone and so were the bartender and the DJ.

He looked at his watch.

Forty-five minutes past curfew. The Mustang Club was dark. Gentle had never seen the place like this. How the hell had this happened? He still felt groggy.

Had he bought something from the fish lady? The old woman came through the Mustang Club a couple of times a night selling round blisters of fish jerky, the size of a slice of bread. If you gave the fish lady some extra won, she'd bring you something from the pharmacy.

You never knew exactly what the fish lady would bring.

But he hadn't taken anything.

Even if she'd been there, Gentle didn't want dope showing up in a random piss-test.

He was too short.

How did they miss him at closing time?

He must have slumped over in the booth. Fallen on the floor.

His eyes were adjusting to the dark. He pulled one of the bar stools out and sat down. Behind the bar, the rows of bottles holding American booze alternated with bottles holding colored water.

He didn't want anything to drink.

The lady bartender lived behind this place.

Probably Sunny #5 had a little place back there too.

He thought about her and the fat-ass lifer at the bar.

It made him sad.

The door wasn't locked from the inside. He opened it a crack, then shut it, seeing the snow still coming down in the alley.

He had a choice to make.

He could sleep here in the bar.

But Kilkenny was right. This was just the kind of thing Major Friend would bust him for.

Or, he could head up to the gate.

Explain, and hope the MP's on duty would let him in.

It was just the kind of thing Friend would nail him for.

There was a third possibility.

Gentle shook his head.

It was brilliant.

He could break on to the base.

Why not?

Who would be on guard?

And on a night like this who would see him?

He stood up.

He needed a beer for the road.

He opened an OB then fished out some money from his wallet and laid it on the bar.

He had his SOFA card in his wallet, too.

The Status of Forces Agreement card was a get-out-of-jail free certificate worked out between the Korean and the American authorities.

He saw eyes behind the bar. He didn't know the bartender kept a cat.

Except it wasn't a cat.

He saw the nametag.

Except the nametag was wrong.

This wasn't Sunny #5.

This was no waitress.

The woman's arms and legs were stretched out.

She wore expensive clothes, her eyes were open, and she was dead.

He had never seen her before.

How long had he slept?

He glanced at his watch.

In the time it took for the minute hand to work its way around the dial everything had changed.

A woman lay dead on the floor.

Gentle squatted next to the body.

He lifted the woman's hand.

It felt heavy.

Shouldn't he feel for her pulse?

He knew it was futile, but he still felt her wrist for a sign of life.

He felt a knot in his chest and tears coming to his eyes.

❋ ❋ ❋

Things started to swim around Gentle.

He was weeping.

Suddenly everything seemed strange and even more foreign.

For a second, he couldn't remember where he was and why he was there.

He heard something.

A car was pulling up outside the bar.

Gentle heard the sound of the engine, two slamming car doors and Korean voices.

He'd been in country for a year and could barely understand a word of Korean.

But he knew they were coming in.

He heard the door shake and then open.

It hadn't been locked.

Gentle dropped the woman's hand.

He needed to hurry. Find a place to hide.

He tried not to breathe.

Gripping the oversized OB bottle he slid from his crouch and low-crawled across the barroom floor, away from the woman's body and into the only place in the club which would provide cover.

The DJ's glass cubicle.

The blind disc jockey had left a pack of cigarettes and a lighter on top of the graphic equalizer.

Gentle picked the lighter up and felt it.

A heavy Zippo.

Gentle concentrated on the lighter.

Mr. Yee had taught him to push fear away like a solid object.

Holding flashlights, the men crossed the room.

The lighter was embossed with something.

Gentle couldn't tell what it was.

Afraid to put it down and make a sound, Gentle slid the lighter into his pocket.

Gentle's eyes had adjusted to the light. The men were getting closer to the bar and closer to discovering the body. He tried to compress his frame in the booth, tried to make himself shorter.

It was impossible.

The two men shined their flashlights into the Naugahyde booth where Gentle had awakened.

Five minutes ago?

Ten?

It seemed longer.

They paid special attention to the booth, as if they expected to find something there.

Were they looking for him?

They spoke quickly and turned away from the booth.

Gentle knew he was being paranoid.

How would these two know he'd passed out in the booth?

Nobody had noticed him. He might have been invisible.

Nobody had even noticed him but Sunny # 5.

And she had left.

The two men walked behind the bar and directed their flash-lights on the body.

The taller man wore a black leather jacket, black leather gloves.

Salt and pepper hair cut short. He looked like he called the shots.

His sidekick was shorter, stockier, and his face was deeply pit-ted with pockmarks.

Don Quixote and Sancho Panza in the Land of the Morning Calm.

They were so close.

Even behind glass, Gentle smelled the men.

They looked at the woman.

The tall man raised his voice, but not appreciably. Gentle couldn't tell if he was surprised.

Gentle heard a metal tap skidding on floor from the toe of the tall man's motorcycle boot.

Gentle's chest tightened. He tried to remember Mr. Yee's breathing directions.

Mr. Yee was fanatical about breathing.

Were the men surprised by the body?

Gentle still couldn't tell. He heard the car running outside the bar.

They weren't planning to be here long.

Just long enough to find me, Gentle thought.

The cubicle wasn't any kind of hiding place at all. The one-way glass of the cubicle would only work if the men didn't look too closely.

They would see him.

They didn't look surprised at all by the corpse.

They would see Gentle and then they would kill him.

He had to do something, and it would have to be done quickly.

He measured the distance to the door.

If he could get past these bastards...

The door was only twenty feet away. No farther. If he could

get past these bastards, he could still use his original plan. He

could break back onto the base, and nobody would be the wiser.

Particularly not Major Friend.

If he could get past these two.

The short one, Sancho Panza, pulled out a gun.

A bad sign.

In this country anyone carrying a gun was a bad guy.

A very, very bad guy.

Don Quixote and Sancho didn't look like cops.

He needed the element of surprise.

Better yet, he needed luck.

A lot of it.

Don Quixote leaned over and put his gloved hand on the

woman's throat, stood up, kicked her body hard in the side.

Gentle needed to get out of there.

Quixote stepped over the body and kicked again.

Hard.

The toe of his motorcycle boot driving into her ribs.

The woman didn't make a sound.

The only sound was the thud of boot against ribs.

Gentle had to do something.

Plan or no plan.

He had to do something.

Sancho Panza walked toward the cubicle.

As quietly as he could, Gentle stood on top of the DJ's chair.

They couldn't see him yet.

The two-way mirror didn't work within a step or two.

They would see him.

Gentle couldn't afford to let them get close to the cubicle.

The lady bartender would find him tomorrow lying in a heap

at the bottom of the cubicle with a bullet in his brain.

Three...

Gentle inhaled deeply. Felt the breath go into his lungs.

Visualized.

Two...

He exhaled, then inhaled again, this time as if to fill his lungs for a deep-sea plunge.

He remembered Mr. Yee's training.

Everything had to do with breath.

Everything.

One...

Gentle held his arm over his eyes and flew through the glass.

What is the sound of breaking glass?

For Gentle, it was the sound of a dream, coming to an end.

Don Quixote turned and Gentle felt the man's nose splinter under the driving impact of his OB bottle slamming upward.

Without hesitating, Gentle wheeled around twice and drove his boot into Sancho Panza's groin.

The shot from the shorter man's gun missed Gentle.

He ran into the alley from the door where the two men had entered.

It was still snowing. The car was running.

* * *

Sounds are muffled in a snowstorm.

The black sedan was the only sound Gentle heard on the street. He jumped into the car, slammed it into gear and floored the accelerator.

He heard the sound of the gun again.

This time it could have been a backfire.

From some other car, maybe.

Not from this beauty.

He took the corner fast. Maybe too fast, in the snow, but things were happening too quickly.

He needed to get back on the base, but he could hardly pull up to the guard shack in this car.

He needed to put some distance between himself and Don

Quixote and Sancho Panza. As far as he knew, they were still in the bar.

He would need to...

A jeep pulled around the corner in front of him. Were the MPs looking for him?

He slammed his foot on the brake and leaned on the steering wheel to avoid the jeep.

The black sedan skidded on ice hidden beneath the snow.

The car went into a free spinning pirouette. Gentle felt weightless.

Once.

Twice...

The car spun a third time before slamming to a stop against a concrete wall. He looked out of the cracked windshield of the sedan. The jeep had stopped and someone was running toward him.

An American.

Gentle didn't have time to check for injuries. He hoped he

wasn't hurt, but he had to get away from the car.

He wasn't just looking at a delay in his DEROS now. He would be looking at prison time.

Leavenworth, if he was lucky.

Prison here, if Korean police got to him first and the SOFA card didn't work its magic.

He stopped.

Even from a distance Gentle recognized Friend. No way he'd turn himself in to Major Friend. The bastard would…

No way would Gentle turn himself in now.

He had to move. Run. Hide.

At least an hour had passed since curfew.

It had to be Friend.

With that walk it couldn't be anyone else. Gentle forced himself from behind the steering wheel.

He had to move.

There had to be a way out. The street was dark and the snow still fell. The air felt colder than a witch's tit.

Just like Holden.

Just like good old Pencey Prep.

Major Friend didn't look like he'd recognized Gentle yet.

Not yet anyway.

But it wouldn't take very long.

Gentle saw an opening to an alley.

He had to get to it. He stood up cautiously. Being tall made Gentle stand out in Korea. He ran toward the alley, feeling the soles of his boots slipping underneath him.

"Gentle…"

Shit.

It *was* Friend.

He'd been spotted.

He refused to turn around.

Ran quickly instead.

"Gentle…" Friend's voice was unmistakable.

The only sound in the snow.

A few feet more and Gentle knew he would get a break. You

could go forever down these alleys. They were mazes even in ideal conditions. He plunged into the dark maw of the alley's opening. He ran until he came to a wall and then turned.

Repeated.

Turned.

Repeated.

Running without the slightest idea where he was going, but knowing he had to get away.

Who knew where he was?

Nobody.

He was lost. The only times he'd been here, he'd been drunk.

He wasn't drunk now.

He felt sober.

When was the last time he heard Friend's voice? He had to be safe now, didn't he?

The memory of Friend's voice receded, like a bad dream.

Gentle kept running through the alley.

He was lost.

If he stopped, they would catch him.

The thought of the two men made him run.

They would track him down. His footprints would give him away.

He needed to stop.

How many turns had he made since he entered the alley?

He had lost track.

A sickening thought occurred to him.

What if I turn the next corner and come back to the car?

He needed to sit down.

Stop.

Rest.

Collect his thoughts.

Thank God for the snow. The snow would cover his tracks.

He would rest.

Sit.

Just for a moment.

What was the name of the Jack London story?

He'd read it in junior high school.

He was freezing his ass off, and he remembered the story.

The Yukon prospector had frozen to death in the snow.

Well, it wasn't quite as cold as that.

Not yet, anyway.

He just needed to sit down for a while and rest.

He stumbled into another blind doorway. This one led into a courtyard. If they caught him in here, there would be no way out. The thought entered his mind, but fatigue dismissed it. In the courtyard, a yellow light bulb illuminated a bicycle covered with snow.

It was the first light he'd seen since entering the alley. He walked toward the light.

Tripped.

Dumping a stack of OB bottles over.

It sounded like a bomb.

Lights went on in the house.

LUMINESCENT HANDS OF HER WATCH

Harmony woke up suddenly and knew she wouldn't be able to go back to sleep. First the screaming woman. How long had she screamed at the man?

Now this crash outside.

The woman had used a combination of Korean and GI obscenities. Harmony could make out a word here and there. Eventually the woman stopped.

Harmony knew she was awake for the night. She hoped the woman was all right. She sounded as if she was yelling at someone. The screams became feverish and then stopped abruptly. How long ago? It seemed like a full night, but it couldn't be. Harmony looked at the luminescent hands of her watch. The second hand moved slowly.

The crash must have been caused by an animal. She heard it

rummaging around outside her door.

A dog maybe? It would be half-frozen.

It was moving closer toward the door.

"Please," Harmony said, "would you please just quiet down?"

MIDNIGHT VACUUM SALESMAN

Gentle kneeled next to the door and knocked tentatively.

No answer.

No surprise.

The woman spoke English. She would be frightened.

Please, he thought.

Open the door.

Knowing she wouldn't open it.

Not for him. Not at this time of night. Not in this freezing weather.

Gentle pushed himself closer to the door, hoping at least some heat would come though the paper-thin veneer of the door.

"Hey," he said.

She could hear him.

Maybe she would listen.

And not scream.

"Hey," he repeated. "My name is Ben Gentle. Spec 4 Ben Gentle."

His name and rank.

The way they advised in training films.

"I've got three days left here before I go home."

He knocked on the door again.

"I need help."

No answer.

Somehow, Gentle knew she was listening.

She had to listen.

"If I get caught out here, I'm in trouble. Bad trouble."

He told the unseen woman about waking up in the bar.

About being chased by the two men.

About being seen by Major Friend.

"You may know him," Gentle said, "he's got it in for me."

Everyone knew Major Friend. And everyone knew Friend was an asshole.

He didn't tell her about Sunny # 5 or about the men who had

TRINITY AND THE SHORT-TIMER

followed him.

They could still be following him.

They probably were.

He stopped talking. It wasn't going to work. She wasn't going to let him in.

And why would she?

He could be a murderer.

He could be a rapist.

He could be a midnight vacuum salesman, a cult recruiter, or a million other things which would stop her from opening the door.

So he would have to sit out here and rest for a while. Then he would move on.

Slowly, carefully, he would make it back to the gate.

And he would scale the fence and work his way through the snow back to the barracks.

It wouldn't be a problem.

Hearing her voice shocked him.

"What can I do?" she said.

He couldn't believe it.

He stopped.

Held his breath.

Had she really spoken?

He whispered.

"Could you please let me in for a few minutes?"

She kept the light off and opened the door.

Just slightly.

"Come in," she said.

He had never seen such a beautiful woman.

YELLOW LINOLEUM

They spoke for a while in the little room with the yellow lino-leum floor.

Harmony gave Gentle a cup of the barley tea and he drank it.

Slowly.

"I can make it," he said. "I know how to get back on base. I could do it in my sleep. It's not a problem."

She could see he was frightened.

It showed on his face and in the way he held the cup of tea be-tween his hands. Harmony watched the cup shake slightly.

Cold, she thought. But mostly he's frightened. What could she do? She looked at her watch.

It was too early. She had gotten some sleep, but not much. She hated the idea of surrendering this room to him.

It was *her* room.

The old man gave it to her.

How long ago was that?

It felt like ages ago.

She remembered leaving Chad on the bus.

Another lifetime.

This was her room.

Harmony pushed one of the hard pillows toward Gentle with her foot. She had changed out of her clothes and was wearing an old nightshirt she'd had forever.

She didn't look glamorous or seductive.

Besides, she trusted him.

She put the pillow under Gentle's slumping head.

He was barely awake.

"I'll go back out in a minute… Just so long as Friend's gone."

"Where's your friend?"

He hadn't said anything about a friend.

But she knew he was only talking in his sleep. His head slumped forward into his hands, knees bent with his elbows resting on them, boots still on.

Sound asleep now.

Sound asleep sitting upright.

Harmony took the empty teacup from his hands and put the heavy quilt around his shoulders.

She looked at him.

He'd said his name was Ben Gentle.

✳ ✳ ✳

He would sleep for a while.

He was nice looking and was intelligent.

He'd spoken politely.

Not at all like Chad.

She had believed him.

She tucked the quilt more snugly around his body and guided him onto the heated floor.

Gentle sighed.

He was tall.

His boots, a little snow still clinging to one, touched the wall.

She patted his shoulder.

She was doing a good turn.

She lay down away from him.

Perpendicular to his body.

Her bare foot barely touching his side.

TOUGH SLEDDING

Korea is called the Land of the Morning Calm.

By morning, Camp Long lay beneath two feet of snow.

Sledding would be tough.

Nobody would be going to the tailor shop. Not in this mess.

Major Stanley Friend stood outside the shop watching the men Mr. Kim sent out with shovels.

They were lighting cigarettes and slapping the snow around like a couple of kids. Friend walked past the men. They usually sat around the tailor shop cross-legged, smoking while they stitched shoes.

At the door, Friend stamped his feet and blew on his hands.

He refused to take off his shoes here.

In the ville, maybe, but not on base.

They were practically on American soil here. They could at least try acting American.

It would be a short visit.

Friend owed Mr. Kim money for the hootch rental.

Mr. Kim eyed Friend with a wary expression.

Like a cat, Friend thought.

Friend picked up one of the magazines Mr. Kim kept in the shop. The GQ's and Esquire magazines served as catalogues for GI clients. They could pick out a suit and Mr. Kim's men would render it in whatever size, fabric, and color could be imagined.

Friend had seen plenty of these suits. They tended to run a little small around the shoulders and short in the crotch.

Friend didn't like the expression on Mr. Kim's face.

What the hell made these Koreans so hard to read?

How much did Mr. Kim know?

Mr. Kim wouldn't know anything.

Then why did Mr. Kim have an I've-got-a-secret look on his face?

What did Mr. Kim know?

Mr. Kim smiled at Friend.

"You don't look so good."

Mr. Kim's expression was matter-of-fact. His voice was flat. His look was placid.

Not looking good?

That was possible. Friend *had* been up most of the night.

PFC Chun had brought him back no later than two.

Friend, out of the goodness of his heart, gave Chun a five dollar bill for his efforts.

Friend wondered what Chun would do with the money.

"You were out too late last night. I think you were forgetting something."

Friend was confused and exasperated. It wasn't the first time he'd been late on the rent for the hootch.

But he'd come to pay the rent.

Nothing more to it.

Was Kim going to play tough now?

"I don't know what you're talking about," Friend said.

Casual.

Like they were discussing the weather.

Friend had come to pay rent.

Why wouldn't he look bad?

Mr. Kim looked pained.

Frustrated.

He could have been explaining calculus to a grade school child.

Friend tried his hands-across-the-water voice.

"What *exactly* are you trying to say, Mr. Kim?"

His voice would have melted butter. It would have reassured anyone.

It was a voice to mend all wounds.

Mr. Kim's face turned red.

"You don't understand?"

Apoplectic red.

"How can you say you don't understand?"

Friend looked around quickly to make sure nobody else was around.

They were alone.

The wrong person overhearing a conversation like this could be dangerous.

"You owe," Mr. Kim said, thrusting his hand forward. "You fucking owe *more*, now."

Nice vocabulary, Friend thought.

And then the terror of the situation hit Friend.

Mr. Kim *knew*.

Friend could tell.

Mr. Kim could get whatever he wanted from Friend.

And what could Friend do about it?

Not a thing.

Friend knew this lecture by heart.

Troops heard it from early in basic training.

Major Friend had *given* the lecture.

Don't get ensnared.

The lecture was usually followed by a DOD movie showing a white mouse getting caught in a trap.

Friend was the mouse.

Mr. Kim moved toward Friend.

Was Mr. Kim going to hit him?

He braced himself, tightening his abdominal muscles.

He wouldn't get caught unprepared.

He pulled out his wallet and held his other up in a stop signal.

"Cool it, Kim." Friend pulled out a clip of bills and held them at Mr. Kim's eye level.

The swat to his hand shocked Friend.

Not a shock of surprise.

A shock.

It felt like an electric current, and it stunned Friend.

The money clip flew across the tailor shop.

A simple backhand.

Friend held his crumpled hand.

He slumped, feeling his eyes swell with tears from Mr. Kim's searing blow.

Could his hand be broken?

Could that even be possible?

Friend held his hand up to his mouth. An electric pulse surged in the arm from his shoulder to the tips of his fingers.

He couldn't move his fingers. He tried, but it hurt too much.

Mr. Kim pushed his index finger into the center of Friend's chest.

"I'm not talking about the fucking rent."

Friend dropped his hand.

He felt as though he had been shot.

How the hell had Kim done that?

He felt a massive pain in his chest.

He'd never felt worse pain.

And then the agony disappeared.

It was as if Kim had the power to start and stop the pain.

Mr. Kim pointed his finger at Friend again.

Smiled.

"You owe me."

Friend blinked back tears.

What the hell was Kim talking about now?

"I got pictures…"

Oh God, Friend thought.

He knows.

He remembered carrying the woman's body into the Mustang Club.

Putting the Mustang Club pin on her.

Why the hell had he done that?

And how did Mr. Kim know?

Maybe he could work a bluff.

Stall for time.

How smart was Kim, anyway?

"I don't know what you're talking about."

"Like shit." Mr. Kim said. "Like fucking shit. My guys got pictures. Maybe you want to see some of them before Seoul gets hold of them."

Pictures.

It was worse than he thought.

Much worse.

Headquarters in Seoul would crucify him.

The wrong pictures would send him to Leavenworth.

Hard time in the Castle.

He held his hand out again.

This time with his palms facing outward toward Kim.

There were things he could do for Kim.

Things Kim had talked to him about before.

Things Friend would never have considered until now.

He had to see the pictures.

See how bad were they?

Damage control.

He hadn't been willing to talk business with Kim before.

But now, the situation was desperate.

Mr. Kim walked back to the desk, pushed aside a swatch of fabric and opened the center drawer. He extracted a legal-sized manila envelope.

Pulled out a sheaf of black and white glossies.

Handed them to Friend.

I'm dead, Friend thought.

"Look at them," Mr. Kim said. "Take a fucking look. They came out nice, don't you think?"

He played with the brad on the end of the envelope. "Of course, these are just prints. You want originals? We can get them for you. No problem. I got them elsewhere."

Of course he had the originals somewhere else.

The son-of-a-bitch.

Friend took a deep breath and took the pictures.

He used his left hand. His right still throbbed.

He thumbed through the pictures quickly, feeling a sense of relief.

Not much relief, but some.

It wasn't the woman.

The photos were grainy. Poor resolution certainly. Like security shots from a ceiling mounted camera at a convenience store.

But they were definitely him.

The figure in the pictures was definitely one Major Stanley

Friend.

And with Friend?

Definitely black market items. Cigarettes. Whiskey. Beer.

Friend receiving money.

He might not be Major Friend any more if these pictures got into the wrong hands.

But they wouldn't send him to Leavenworth.

Busted, no doubt, but prison time?

Probably not.

He couldn't believe he actually felt relieved.

Things could be worse.

He looked up from the pictures into Mr. Kim's face.

The tailor's expression was one of studied indifference.

He drummed the table, his fingers making a regular rhythmic pattern against the top.

It drove Friend crazy.

He's got me where he wants me.

Why doesn't he say something?

"So, Mr. Kim."

As if he'd just been pulled over by a state trooper.

"You've always been reasonable. Isn't there any way we can reach a little understanding?"

Mr. Kim shook his head slightly.

"You know what we want," he said.

Smile and drummed his fingers.

"Think about that, Major Friend."

NOT SERGEANT ROCK

Coffee kept him going.

From the first formation in the morning until the first beer after work, Staff Sergeant Milt Kilkenny rarely could be seen without the mug in his hands.

He never washed the coffee mug, which came from a savings and loan in Erie, a few miles from his hometown.

He didn't plan on washing the mug until his last day in country.

The mug was starting to obtain a nice patina.

Probably some micro-organisms too, but who the hell really cared?

Gentle hadn't shown up for formation this morning.

Of course, this wasn't the stateside army.

Things here were a little more lax.

And Kilkenny liked Gentle.

He wouldn't hesitate to cover for him if Major Friend asked

any questions.

But it bothered him, nevertheless.

He thought Gentle was going to cool it.

Gentle was short, and the last thing he needed to do was mess around this close to departure.

Nothing would please Major Friend more than to bust Gentle on the last day of his tour.

Friend was just the kind of hard-ass who would do it.

Kilkenny sipped his coffee and looked around the motor pool office. A pile of mail and a shelf of preventive maintenance manuals.

Gentle was bored as hell down here.

There was nothing to do.

The Korean civilians took care of the vehicles.

Mostly, Gentle sat around and read.

And not Sergeant Rock cartoons or western paperbacks, either.

Gentle read serious looking books.

Gentle was smart.

Kilkenny had a bad feeling.

Where the hell was Gentle?

Sutherland wouldn't know, but Kilkenny asked him anyway.

Sutherland could barely move. He was a walking hangover.

"You down at the ville last night?"

Sutherland scowled.

"See Gentle?"

A shrug of the shoulders.

Sutherland didn't see anything.

Even sober, Sutherland couldn't find his ass with a flashlight and a head start.

"Back in a minute," Kilkenny said.

If Sutherland heard him, he didn't say anything to prove it.

Maybe Gentle was still at the barracks.

He could call over there, but what the hell.

The drive from the motor pool took about a minute.

He would have driven, except for the snow.

Staff Sergeant Kilkenny should have been a Sergeant First Class.

Maybe a First Sergeant.

He would have been at least a SFC if not for a string of bad luck early in his career.

None of the events were his fault, but his career was permanently on hold.

* * *

Kilkenny walked into the Quonset hut.

No sound.

Walked toward Gentle's bunk.

Probably simply a matter of dragging Gentle out of his bunk.

Kilkenny wasn't bitter about his stalled career, and he had never taken up full-time drinking.

He'd watched too many men become booze-hounds.

Kilkenny rarely thought about his bad breaks.

What could he do about it anyway?

Sure, he'd been disgusted.

Who wouldn't be?

He almost left the Army entirely.

Then he came to his senses.

It would have been ignorant to get out before earning his pension.

And SSGT Kilkenny wasn't dumb.

He wouldn't let the bastards win twice.

He had less than two years before retirement.

Only one after he got back stateside.

He could do two years standing on his head.

He couldn't fathom doing anything else.

He had plans for retirement.

He would go home.

He would have enough money to fish and hunt and generally do what he damn well pleased.

Kilkenny's experience gave him a different outlook on Army life.

Kilkenny knew the book. He could quote Army regulations with the best.

But nothing disgusted him more than blind adherence to authority.

In Kilkenny's view, men like Major Friend were the worst.

Legalistic, vindictive, and without a shred of credibility.

❊ ❊ ❊

Gentle's bunk was empty.

It hadn't changed since last night.

The plain GI wool blanket was stretched tight across the bunk.

Gentle hadn't slept here.

Kilkenny knew he couldn't let Friend find out.

Friend would happily bust Gentle.

Kilkenny grabbed the top of the blanket near the pillow.

Tugged it down to the center of the bunk.

The unmade bunk now looked just like the others in the

Quonset hut.

None of the troops made up their bunks.

This wasn't the stateside Army.

The cleaning woman did it for them when she got there.

Now it looked like Gentle spent the night in the barracks.

With any luck, Gentle would show up in the motor pool this morning.

"Everything normal here, Sergeant Kilkenny?"

Kilkenny stopped.

His hand were still on the blanket.

He knew the voice.

Friend.

Standing in the doorway.

He'd seen Kilkenny mess up Gentle's bunk.

"Just thought I'd stop over into the barracks. See what's up with the soldiers."

Bullshit, Kilkenny thought.

Friend didn't care about the troop welfare.

Friend only cared about Friend.

Kilkenny straightened up.

Dropped the edge of the blanket.

"Everything's copacetic, sir... Strange though..."

"What's strange, Sergeant Kilkenny?"

Kilkenny didn't like him.

Didn't like his way of talking like there was a pole up his ass.

He didn't like Friend.

He would be damned if he'd let Friend bury Gentle.

"Strange the woman hasn't gotten here and taken care of these bunks."

Friend slapped his gloves together. Starting to take one of them off.

"What's really strange is Gentle going to the ville last night. Isn't he heading home?"

Kilkenny saw the trap.

There wasn't any right answer.

Major Friend made the rules.

No overnights the last week.

It was a chickenshit rule, but it was Friend's rule.

Friend had seen Kilkenny pulling Gentle's blanket down.

"How about if we have a chat, Sergeant Kilkenny?"

Kilkenny felt a slow burn creep over his face.

"How about if we don't, Major?"

Insubordination.

Kilkenny knew it as soon as he said it.

But Friend ignored Kilkenny's remark.

"Gentle didn't report this morning?"

Kilkenny shrugged.

"He's doing his checklist, I expect. The usual bullshit."

Friend shook his head.

"Don't count on it. But if he did stay out, don't write him up."

Kilkenny wasn't sure he had heard correctly.

"Right sir."

Friend smile almost looked genuine.

"Cut him some slack... He's too short to bother with."

Kilkenny watched Friend move to the door.

Friend turned before leaving.

"Don't write him up," he said. "Just send him to my office."

BAD COMPANY

The Run-in-Chef consisted of some tables, a couple of pinball machines and a jukebox.

The stainless steel kitchen served American food and the fridge was stocked with beer and soda.

Trinity sat away from the jukebox, waiting for his order of bacon, eggs, and grits.

PFC Sutherland slumped over the pinball machine.

Bad Company blaring from the jukebox.

The road crew had worked hard this morning. Most of the snow was cleaned up. It looked good out there.

He wondered about Caleb Henderson. Why was he here?

What happened to his son?

In hindsight, Trinity realized he should have asked more questions.

Maybe he could have helped.

He'd been overwhelmed by the war hero.

Who expected to see Caleb Henderson?

SFC Milt Kilkenny came into the place and pulled up the chair next to Trinity.

"Mind if I sit down, Mr. Trinity?"

Trinity pointed toward one of the empty seat.

He liked Kilkenny.

Kilkenny was a good guy.

A pleasure to be around.

The eggs and grits were brought to the table. Trinity buttered the grits and shook on salt and pepper.

"Nice breakfast," Kilkenny said. "That's the way I like them."

He turned toward Sutherland and shook his head.

"Thought I left him back at the motor pool," he said.

A half of a smile crossed Trinity's face. He reached for the Gunslinger hot sauce.

"Roads are good?"

Kilkenny lowered his voice.

Sutherland was racking up a score on the machine.

"I got a problem, Frank."

Trinity wasn't surprised. Trinity heard lots of problems. He hoped Kilkenny's problem wasn't too difficult.

"It's one of the troops, Frank. He's a short-timer. You've seen him around."

Kilkenny described Gentle. He hadn't reported to the motor pool.

"It's not the worst thing in the world," Kilkenny said. "You know that."

He looked over at Sutherland. Shook his head again.

"But it is if you're a couple of days short, and the old man already has it in for you."

Trinity understood.

Trinity worked with both commissioned officers and enlisted soldiers. His sympathies nearly always lay with the enlisted man.

"He went down to the ville. I'm sure of it," Kilkenny said. "I wasn't there, but that's where he would have gone."

"What time?"

"Maybe eight? Nine?"

Kilkenny shrugged.

"We talked for a few minutes. He said he wasn't going, but I know he went."

"Does he have a girlfriend down there?"

"Christ, Trinity, I don't think so. Gentle sticks to himself. You know the rules, though. Friend will slaughter him."

Trinity knew the rules.

Friend was known for imposing arbitrary rules and reversing them within days.

Men like Kilkenny had to either enforce the rules or turn a blind eye.

Trinity looked out the window of the Run-in-Chef. Hard to believe the dump of snow yesterday.

It was clear and the sky was blue.

The base was alive.

Trinity took a sip of coffee.

"Did you see the old man walking around the base yesterday? The one with the beard and the blue coat."

"Sure," Kilkenny said. "He must have gone around the perimeter two or three times.

Trinity put down the coffee mug.

"Cal Henderson."

Kilkenny stared.

"You're shitting me."

"I'm not."

Kilkenny shook his head.

"Well I'll be fucked."

Trinity grinned.

"You see him today, you might want to offer him a ride."

"No shit."

"Not that he'd take it."

"Cal Henderson?" Kilkenny pointed toward the window.

"The one that…"

"The same one. He's looking for his son."

Kilkenny stood up. "He looks like he's eighty years old…"

"He's doing all right though, considering."

Kilkenny shoved his chair under the table. "Can you keep your eye out for Gentle? Maybe give him a little talk?"

"Sure, Milt," Trinity said, "I'll keep my eyes open."

"Thanks, Frank. He's a good kid. I'd hate to see him get screwed."

"I'll see what I can do."

"Strictly on the QT, right?"

"Of course."

Trinity knew any inquiries would have to be discreet.

Kilkenny trusted him.

Trinity watched Kilkenny leave.

Kilkenny was the heart and soul of the army.

Trinity would find Gentle as a favor to Kilkenny.

UNDISCIPLINED, UNMILITARY, PROBABLY UNPATRIOTIC

Major Stanley Friend looked around the office.

Everything tidy, everything in its place.

Kim wouldn't make any trouble. He couldn't expose any of Friend's activities without implicating himself.

As bad as Leavenworth might be, Korean prison would be ten times worse.

Friend decided he had nothing to worry about.

At least from Mr. Kim.

He leaned back in his chair and crossed his arms in self-satisfaction.

Only one thing bothered him.

One, tiny little thing.

He leaned forward in the desk chair.

Why hadn't he thought of it?

All Kim's bullshit meant nothing.

Did Gentle know anything?

It was possible.

Gentle wasn't dumb.

Undisciplined, unmilitary, probably unpatriotic.

But he wasn't dumb.

How hard would it be for the son-of-a-bitch to do a little checky-checky?

Not hard at all. Would Spec 4 Gentle appreciate the chance to screw over Major Stanley Friend?

You'd better believe it.

The phone rang.

Friend leaned forward and picked it up on the second ring.

Mr. Kim's voice.

"Major Friend? I think you might want to come back over to

the shop."

Friend shook his head.

Scowled.

What the hell did Kim want now?

They were settled.

"Sorry, Kim. No can do. I'm a little tied up. I don't expect to be able to…"

Mr. Kim cut him off.

"Listen, Friend. You better come take a look. We found something. You might want to see it too."

Friend put down the phone.

They found *something*.

Something could insure hard time in Leavenworth.

❊ ❊ ❊

Mr. Kim drummed his fingers against his desk.

Friend looked at the Polaroid pictures Kim handed to him, keeping them at chest level, sheathing them like a poker hand.

Was it safe in here?

Of course not. Kim ran a business. Anyone could come into the tailor shop right now.

They would see Friend holding enough visual evidence to send him to prison for life.

American prison if he was lucky.

Maybe Korean prison.

Kim put his other hand on the desk and rolled his fingers.

Kim's left hand went tap tap tap tap TAP while his right hand went tap TAP tap TAP tap TAP.

How the hell did he do that?

The son-of-a-bitch was grinning.

Friend looked at the large pair of shears sitting on the tailor's desk.

Close enough to pick up and drive through Kim's heart.

Tap tap tap tap TAP.

Friend felt his hand throb.

Tap TAP tap TAP tap TAP.

He might get his hand half way to the shears, but Kim would pull them away just in time.

Or he would use them on Friend.

"Well, you got a decision yet?"

Kim looked pleased with himself.

The pictures were all he needed.

There wasn't any point wondering how Kim got them.

The pictures themselves were benign.

They showed Friend and the woman at a restaurant, at a bar, and walking together.

Tame stuff.

But enough to show Friend knew the woman.

Had some sort of relationship with her.

From there, any investigator could place her with Friend at the time of her death.

"Just a minute," Friend said. "Let me think."

"Not much to think about, is there Major Friend?"

Friend shook his head.

Kim was right.

There was nothing more to think about.

How much more trouble could he get into, if he went along with Kim's plan?

Not much more.

Only a life sentence or two.

With time off for good behavior he could be out in time to see the Tigers home opener in 2057.

The base armory was part of Friend's responsibility.

And it wasn't as if Kim was some sort of North Korean agent.

The way Kim described it, he had friends who found Korea's gun laws restrictive.

There wasn't much to the operation. It would be no more difficult than black marketing a few lousy stereo systems.

Any soldier could turn a profit from selling a few items here and there.

Friend's involvement would be minimal.

An unlocked office, an unattended key...

Presto...

No more problems.

The woman's accident would never be reported.

Mr. Kim would take care of it.

Friend could return to the states without a care in the world.

Major Friend looked at the shears. He wanted to stab Mr. Kim.

Again he felt the throbbing pain Kim inflicted upon him earlier.

The pain was real.

He leaned toward Kim.

Took his eyes off the shears.

"Tell me what I need to do," he said.

FERAL CATS

Harmony woke up first and saw Gentle.

He was still asleep.

She remembered why he was in her room.

She remembered the knock on the door. Gentle's calm and sincere voice.

Not frantic or hostile like Chad would have been.

Chad.

Where would he be now? Undoubtedly he would have awakened on the bus. His head would be throbbing, and he would look around for Harmony.

He liked to complain early in the morning.

The thought of Chad looking for her on the bus made Harmony smile.

Though Chad would never admit it, Harmony's limited command of Korean was better than Chad's.

Chad would get nowhere with the bus driver. With his temper, she thought, he'll be lucky if he doesn't get thrown off the bus.

She hoped he'd slept soundly, each minute carrying him farther and farther away from her.

Gentle turned over in his sleep and extended his arm over his head.

His sleeping face was exposed.

He's handsome, she thought.

He has an intelligent face.

He hadn't panicked, even during a crisis.

He was the opposite of Chad.

She liked him and she was glad she had been able to help him.

She stood and stretched. She pulled the sleep shirt tightly around her shoulders and rummaged through her backpack for her Irish cable knit.

She ran a brush through her hair. Why didn't she go ahead and have it cut?

The morning felt cold. An icy draft came in through the

window. She took the tongs from the corner of the room and dropped another of the round charcoal bricks into the stove.

Thankfully the window had been cracked open. It must have been the old man. She didn't remember doing it.

She had been so tired when she got the room.

She remembered almost nothing before she fell asleep.

She remembered the woman screaming. At first, while still asleep, she'd thought it was an animal.

Maybe feral cats.

Gentle had come to the door. Not immediately, but soon after the screaming.

She looked at him again.

Was it possible the woman had been screaming at him? Of course it was possible, but Harmony didn't really believe it.

She shook her head.

It wasn't possible.

She was a better judge of character than that.

She thought she was.

She would have said she was.

But she'd fallen for Chad.

What had she seen in him?

Chad had sounded intelligent.

He was handsome in a rumpled way.

She looked at Gentle.

Could he be another Chad?

She put the kettle, still filled with last night's barley tea, back onto the electric burner.

This one looked intelligent and handsome.

More handsome and more intelligent than Chad.

Was that a good sign or a bad sign?

She ran her finger down the side of the leather jacket he'd left near his head.

It didn't matter.

She was only helping him.

As soon as he woke up, she would get him out the door.

The snow had stopped falling and the morning sun was bright.

As soon as he left, she would put on her own backpack and head out.

She hoped the driver didn't tell Chad the name of the town.

But that didn't matter either.

She wouldn't stay long enough for Chad to track her down.

She would take the first bus to Seoul.

She would show her passport and buy a ticket back to the states.

Her savings would cover the flight.

She could imagine the questions she would be asked.

She would have a hundred stories.

But for now, her Korean adventure was coming to an end.

JOHNNY HORTON AT THE MUSTANG

“One more stop,” Trinity said.

He was driving today.

Mr. Yee, riding shotgun didn’t look entirely comfortable being the passenger.

Mr. Yee often looked uncomfortable.

"I know this guy, Gentle," he said.

Trinity parked next to the crumbling brick side of the Mustang Club.

"One of your students?" Trinity said.

Yee nodded.

"He's good. He's a good guy, too."

They stood outside the club.

Cold as hell out.

"Let's go find him," Trinity said.

* * *

The snow was already black near the wall.

There was no sign outside the bar.

No gaudy neon like the streets in Itaewon.

Just a courtyard.

A small dog on a chain in front of the door.

A stack of empty OB bottles as high as the door.

The Mustang Club opened early.

Camp Long had shift workers.

Stateside do-gooders never had succeeded in making these places off limits.

Trinity pushed the door open with his boot.

The music had already started.

In the glass corner cubicle, the blind disc jockey cranked up a Johnny Horton song about Alaska.

The lights were low and the volume was high.

Inside, it could have been eleven at night as easily as eleven in the morning.

Morning meant country music. Music for lifers.

The only American was a wide load perched on a stool at the end of the bar.

Mr. Yee came in after Trinity.

He looked uncomfortable.

He gazed around the dark room as though measuring for drapes.

Trinity asked for a Coke.

The woman put the Coke in front of him and slid a can of Schlitz in front of Mr. Yee.

Mr. Yee grabbed the can as it went by.

Just like in the movies, Trinity thought.

Still looking uncomfortable, Mr. Yee cracked open the Schlitz.

Trinity put a bill in front of the bartender.

Enough to cover the Coke, the beer, and then some.

He knew it wasn't necessary.

He pushed Gentle's picture forward.

The bartender smiled.

She was middle aged, but the gold edges of her front teeth

made her look older.

"I know him."

She passed the photograph back to Trinity. He stuffed it back under the sheep-drover's jacket, into his shirt pocket. No sense making a production out of things. The photo was taken early in Gentle's tour.

Gentle was a kid.

Mr. Yee drank the Schlitz from the can, eyes fixed on the display of bottles behind the bar.

The beer was black-market, of course.

So were the elaborately displayed bottles of Jim Beam and Black Velvet.

Only the mysterious bottles of Korean wine, and the OB beers were legit.

That wasn't Trinity's department.

Leave that to Major Friend.

"Last night?"

Trinity expected the bartender to cooperate. He expected

she would lead him down one of the myriad alleys behind the place where they would find Gentle fast asleep in a hooch.

Probably hungover.

Instead, the woman shook her head.

"He was only here for a while."

She held her hands up.

A shrug.

How could she possibly remember all of the comings and goings of any night?

Trinity understood.

The bartender couldn't help him.

But Gentle had been here.

Trinity stood up and thanked her.

The bartender's face hardened.

"You know Major Friend?"

Trinity cocked his head.

"I know him."

She made a guttural sound.

"Major Friend is number fucking ten."

Mr. Yee put down the beer.

Put his coat on.

"Time to go, Trinity."

The blind DJ started a new song.

Styx.

"*The Grand Illusion*."

A little early for that to come out, Trinity thought.

But it was a long song, and the DJ looked like he was taking a break.

Outside, Trinity stopped on the sidewalk in front of the car.

He turned to Mr. Yee.

"You go ahead and take an early afternoon. I'm going to do a little checking."

Trinity knew Mr. Yee would be more than happy to take the afternoon off.

Trinity put the collar up on his sheep-drover's jacket.

The day was bright.

Bright, and bitterly cold.

He decided to walk for a while before getting back into the Impala.

Without a chance to melt, the snow would stay on the ground even though it had stopped falling.

Trinity walked to the back of the Mustang Club.

The alley smelled like an outhouse.

He turned right.

Following his instincts.

Walked a few paces.

Odds were good Gentle walked this way last night.

He kept walking.

There was no pattern to the alley.

It was a labyrinth.

He slowed his pace.

Trinity didn't even have to turn around to know he was being followed.

* * *

He turned and the footsteps stopped.

Nobody there.

Starting again, Trinity heard the steps again.

Again.

Trinity took a quick right at the next corner. The little alley-way was barely big enough to contain him.

He walked a few steps farther.

He crouched in back of a short wall.

The alley was dark.

He waited.

The steps had been steady and regular.

They would start again soon.

Trinity held his breath.

It didn't take long. The same pattern.

He didn't want to give away his position by looking. The steps sounded heavy though.

Like a man's steps.

Closer.

Almost to the wall.

Trinity lunged forward and grabbed the man, wrapping his arm around his throat and pushing his knee into the small of the man's back.

Trinity heard a grunt. Turned the man's head toward him, then threw him to the side.

"What the hell were you...?"

The DJ shook his head.

Stammered.

"Sorry, I needed to talk to you but..."

Trinity felt his own face turn red.

The DJ.

The guy was blind.

Trinity could have killed him.

"You needed to talk to me?"

Why hadn't he just signaled to Trinity back at the Mustang Club?

"Sorry," the DJ said, "I'll be in big trouble."

"Talk."

"The GI you were talking about? He was asleep. In the bar."

How did the guy even know who we were talking about? Trinity wondered.

The Johnny Horton song had been full blast and the DJ was behind a wall of glass on the other side of the room.

"They were talking after you left. I know the man you're looking for."

The DJ was struggling to make himself understood.

"He is a nice man."

"He was asleep?"

"Until I finished."

No use wondering how he knew.

The guy probably knew everything that went on in the place.

"He was still there. Under the table."

The DJ wasn't old. Trinity guessed the man wasn't in his thirties yet. His hair was spiked and the jacket he wore was too thin for the weather.

"What else?" Trinity said.

There had to be something.

"She was lying to you. She knew that guy was there."

"What else?"

It would have been better to interview the DJ inside.

Trinity thought of the noodle shop where he'd talked to Cal Henderson last night.

Better there than in the dim light in this alley.

He was freezing.

The DJ started to shake.

"Take your time," Trinity said. "There's something else, too."

A flake of snow, dry, and no bigger than a fleck of dust fell.

Not that again, Trinity thought.

The DJ was trying to decide.

"She knew," he said. "She knew he was there."

Trinity looked at the DJ. He'd risked something by telling Trinity this much.

Who could say what else he knew?

Trinity knew the DJ wouldn't tell him anything more.

Another flake of snow.

HARMONY

Gentle watched Harmony pull the cheese and salami from her backpack and dig around for her Swiss army knife.

She cut the hard cheddar into cubes, and sliced the salami through its wrinkled paper wrapper.

She really is beautiful, Gentle thought.

It wasn't his imagination at work last night.

He watched her add another brick to the charcoal fire.

She was just as beautiful as she had looked when she opened the door for him the night before. Her blonde hair fell to the sweater she had put on over her night shirt.

"Where do you come from?" Gentle said.

She turned towards him.

He was sitting cross-legged next to the door.

She laughed.

"My father and mother moved around a lot. You could say they're old hippies. They raised us in an old school bus between British Columbia and Washington.

"You're Canadian?"

"My father is. They've more or less settled north of San Francisco." She held up the cheese. "Near Mendocino. That's where this comes from. It's the last of my Christmas care package."

"They named you Harmony."

She laughed.

"It could have been..."

"It's a beautiful name," he said. "It fits you."

"That's nice," she said. "Thanks for saying that."

She swatted him on the leg and handed him a small paper plate with some of the salami and cheese.

"What about you, Mr. Ben Gentle? What's the story with your name?"

Gentle shook his head.

"They named me before the show came out. I was running

around the house in my underwear by then."

"Thanks for not doing that now, by the way."

"You're welcome," he said.

"So then the show comes out," she said, "and you're stuck."

"Exactly…" Gentle said. "But numerologically I was set."

"Numerologically?"

"That's a word, isn't it? You know, how many syllables in a person's name? You should know about that."

She laughed.

"Just because my parents lived in a bus doesn't make us gypsies."

He laughed.

She laughed.

Suddenly she looked serious.

"Are you in trouble?" she said.

"Depends," he said. "It depends how long I'm gone and who notices."

"Won't you be late for something? Reveille?"

"Reveille?"

He laughed. "Oh right. That's what we do before we go out on cavalry charges."

Gentle saw the look on her face and instantly regretted his sarcasm.

"OK, wrong word," she said. "Formation? Mail call?"

"It's all right," he said. "I'm fine. I've got orders sending me home in three days."

Suddenly he was a soldier again.

"What can they do to me now?"

He was trying to convince himself.

"Where's home for you?" she said.

He really didn't think that he'd ever seen such a beautiful woman.

Her wide open blue eyes registered surprise at his answers.

How had this happened?

And what could he do?

He was leaving in three days.

"Middle of Illinois," he said. "It's flat. Come to think of it, that school bus of yours may have been built near our farm."

"You have a farm?"

"Barely. We have a few fields leased. My mother is a teacher. My father died when I was little."

"Sorry," she said. "Who's your friend? You kept talking about him in your sleep."

"Friend?"

"Friend this, friend that. You were pretty distraught."

He shook his head.

"Major Friend. From the base."

"Are you looking forward to going home? You must be excited. Only three days?"

He was glad that she changed the subject.

He shrugged.

"I thought that I would be more excited, to tell you the truth. I mean, that's the whole build-up over here. People have these short-timer calendars... It's a big deal. Almost like your whole life goes into suspended animation here. Then you go back to the states and your real life resumes. It's weird. But all I could think last night was that I felt like Holden Caulfield."

"Turn around," she said.

"What?"

Her voice took on a do-not-disobey tone.

"Just turn around."

He turned around. She looked at his head from the front to the back. She kneeled so close to him that he could smell her.

A nice talcum smell.

"What was that all about?"

"You," she said. "Not a speck of gray. Holden was prematurely gray."

He touched the back of his head.

"You're not Holden." she said. "You can't be. So you need a different literary model."

"Any suggestions?"

"Let's see… Too young for James Bond. And too midwestern."

"Hamlet?"

"You're too decisive. You took the cheese with zero hesitation. Hamlet would have worried that I was in league with Claudius."

"You'd make a good Ophelia," he said.

"Flatterer."

She squinted and drew her head back from him.

"Maybe you could be Huckleberry Finn. You're on the run. Major Friend could be Injun Joe..."

"Pap Finn," Gentle said.

"Right, Pap... So now we should be staging your funeral."

He liked her.

No, he was head over heels.

He looked at her again. He would be gone in three days.

He had to act quickly.

He ruled out an offer of marriage.

"Do you like doughnuts?"

"I happen to love doughnuts."

He held up the mug of barley tea.

Stone cold.

"I know a place…"

She laughed again. He loved the sound of her laughter.

All right, he thought. So he'd had a bad night.

A nightmare.

But the sun was up outside and shining, and he'd lived through everything.

He would be heading home in a few days.

The men with the gun wouldn't be looking for him.

He'd met the most beautiful girl in the world, and she wanted to go out with him for doughnuts.

So what if he lost a stripe?

He wouldn't care if he lost them all.

He would survive.

It was late in the day.

He had slept for a long time.

"I'd love to," she said.

"Sorry?"

"I thought I heard an invitation," she said. "For doughnuts."

"You want to go?"

A smile crept across her face.

"Of course I would, Huckleberry."

She took his hand and held it.

"Give me a second first," she said. "I should get dressed."

SOUL FOOD

Trinity could easily have gone through the regular line at the mess hall. He could have taken a tray and been served the same food.

He liked paying for the dining room service. It only cost a dollar to sit in the private room on the side of the mess hall and a waitress would come and bring him his food and coffee

Definitely worth a buck.

Today was soul food. Trinity confronted the enormous pig's foot in front of him, flanked by a hunk of corn bread, some greens and black-eyed peas.

The pig's foot took up a large portion of the plate.

Soul food was the best thing the mess hall did.

He reached for the bottle of Tabasco.

"You like that, Trinity?" Deavers, the mess sergeant, stood next to the table, an ash forming on the end of his cigarette.

Trinity cut into the pork skin, exposing the meat on the hock.

"It's good, Spoon," Trinity said. "I might need a bigger one though."

Deavers laughed.

"She brought you what you need. You want more, just let me know."

"I eat like this, I'll need two seats on the plane home."

"Nobody got fat off soul food, Trinity."

SSGT Kilkenny came in and took off his hat and field jacket.

Trinity watched Kilkenny until the staff sergeant made eye contact with him.

Trinity wordlessly signaled him.

Deavers glanced at Kilkenny then turned toward Trinity.

"You find your man?"

"Which one?"

"The man in the snow. You and your sidekick were looking for him last night. You find him?"

Cal Henderson.

"Found him," Trinity said. "No worse for the wear."

The waitress filled his coffee again.

Kilkenny sat down.

Deavers put out his cigarette.

"Well, got to get back to it."

"Lunch is good," Trinity said.

Deavers had left.

"Looks good," Kilkenny said.

"Why does Friend have it in for Gentle?"

Kilkenny shrugged. "Got me. Something about the kid gets him."

"I didn't find him. But something's up, that's for sure."

"Christ, Trinity. The kid's got three days to get out of the country. He's getting out of the service. What the hell?"

"I know."

Trinity opened a cup of half and half and stirred it into the coffee.

"I thought I was getting mugged down in the ville, asking about him."

"Was he there?"

"Apparently snoozing under a bar stool. Bartender saw him, but didn't want me to know about it. She let him sleep past curfew."

Kilkenny shook his head. "Most times they do a sweep before last call."

"Not last night."

Kilkenny leaned forward.

"I'll tell you what else is strange."

Trinity sipped the coffee.

Opened another half and half.

"I shoulda told you this earlier. It was right before I saw you. Why I asked you to look into it."

Kilkenny didn't look comfortable.

"Told me what?"

"Friend. I'd just seen him in the barracks. Never seen Friend *there* before. He could see Gentle hadn't been in."

Trinity knew the rule.

"Friend tells me if Gentle comes in I should cut him some slack. I should send him to see him."

"Send Gentle to Major Friend? Friend said that?"

"It spooked me the way he said it."

Kilkenny didn't spook easily, but this had him rattled.

"You think that Friend is up to something?"

Kilkenny hesitated.

"Hell yes, I think he's up to something.."

He stopped.

"I think the bastard has something planned."

"Anything else you think I should know?"

"Gentle's a good kid. I think Friend is dirty."

"Dirty?"

"Dirty," Kilkenny said. "I got no idea what it is, but he's dirty."

Trinity raised his eyebrows.

Kilkenny pulled a cigarette from his fatigue shirt pocket and lit it.

"It's a hunch. I been around... I've seen his type before."

The waitress came back with coffee. Trinity shook her off.

He stood up and put on his coat and hat.

"I'll see if I can find him," he said. "I don't think we talked about anything besides the food today, did we?

Kilkenny exhaled a plume of smoke.

"No sir, I don't think we did. Always a pleasure, though."

Outside the mess hall, Trinity buttoned the jacket.

Snow was starting to come down again.

WARM DOUGHNUTS

Gentle felt good being outside, walking down the street in the snow with Harmony next to him.

He couldn't stop looking over at her. Seeing if she was still there.

There she was in her blue jeans, hiking boots, a nylon shell covering the cable knit sweater.

She'd pulled a beret over her hair and the black wool was covered with snow.

She carried her own backpack. She'd refused his offer to carry it for her.

"It's right around here," he said.

He hoped the doughnut place was nearby.

He thought it was around here, but the streets were confusing.

"You're sure?" she said.

They were close to the bus station.

She would get on the bus and go to Seoul and take an airplane to the other side of the world.

Of course Gentle would be leaving too, but who could say if he'd ever see her again?

She walked closely at his side.

She found the tearoom before he did.

The smell of the doughnuts coming from the packed tearoom was unmistakable.

They took off their coats and hung them on the backs of the only empty chairs. Two older women stood behind the glass counter.

Gentle was hungry.

He started to make hand gestures, pointing toward the dough-nuts.

Harmony laughed.

She spoke quickly to the women, pointing not just to the doughnuts but also to Gentle.

The women were laughing also.

One of them pointed at Gentle, apparently saying something about his height.

Harmony reached up and put her hand on the top of his head.

Gentle smiled at the women. Being with Harmony made him feel better than he had felt for a while.

Harmony turned to Gentle.

"She says that you are one tall man. She wonders how you fit in a car."

She giggled.

"At least that's what I understood. My Korean isn't good."

"It's a hell of a lot better than mine," he said.

He took one of the warm doughnuts the woman had put on a plate.

He felt very tall and very American going back to the table.

The woman had given them two forks.

He held up one of them.

"For the doughnuts," Harmony said.

"Forks?"

Harmony looked at him. "For the doughnuts."

The coffee was instant. The woman brought the boiling water

to their table in two cups and put the freeze-dried crystals in for Harmony and Gentle.

Harmony took the spoon and slowly stirred Gentle's coffee.

"You're sure you're not in trouble?"

He *wasn't* sure.

"No," he said. "A few hours one way or the other isn't going to make any difference."

"I'm glad," she said. "I wouldn't want you to get into trouble on your last day."

"Close," he said. "I've got a couple more days."

He wished, for the first time since he had arrived in Korea that he had more time.

"What are your plans?"

She stirred her own coffee.

"I don't know," she said. "I'll go to the station and find out the bus schedule for Seoul."

"It's bad out there," he said. "Maybe you should stay another night."

She threw her hair back.

"Well, it certainly was exciting last night."

She looked at him.

"What's wrong?" she said. "You didn't..."

He signaled her with his hand to come close.

It was a quick gesture.

Almost desperate.

He put his hands on top of hers, held his head close to hers and whispered.

"We've got to get out of here."

She looked startled. He saw the surprise in her face.

"I'm sorry," he said. "I'll explain later. It's not safe here."

"Come on then," she said.

"Quickly."

He grabbed her jacket and his own and grabbed her backpack.

He couldn't be sure if the men from the Mustang Club had seen him.

Don Quixote and Sancho Panza drank coffee on the other side

of the room.

Gentle and Harmony moved quickly to the door.

The tall one, Don Quixote, was doing the talking.

"Run," Gentle said.

They came out of the tearoom together, the snow hitting them in the face.

"What was that all about?" Harmony said.

Gentle grabbed her arm and pulled her toward the street.

A taxi pulled up and Gentle moved quickly

"Tell you later."

He got into the back seat of the taxi.

An orange Hyundai Pony.

The woman was right.

He barely fit.

"This better be good," Harmony said.

"Kamshida, Atishee," Gentle said.

The driver smiled and reached for his pack of cigarettes.

Through the snow Gentle could see the door of the tearoom

opening.

Don and Sancho were halfway across the street.

Coming toward them.

MR. YEE'S PART OF TOWN

Mr. Yee looked forward to an early afternoon with his wife.

What was Trinity checking?

Who could say?

Yee liked Trinity. Turn-over of investigators was a fact of life, but Trinity was the best Yee had ever worked with.

Still, sometimes Trinity did strange things.

Maybe because Trinity was a cowboy.

Trinity told Yee he really was not a cowboy. He'd said it more than once, but Yee didn't believe him.

Didn't Trinity come from the west?

Didn't he wear a cowboy hat and boots?

Mrs. Yee liked him too. Trinity's easy courtesy impressed her. He wasn't uncivilized like some Americans.

The snow was coming down again. It was going to accumulate, no doubt about that. Yee slowed the car down to a crawl.

Officially he was still on duty.

He needed to keep his eyes open. There was a lot of snow.

Maybe a walk with Mrs. Yee wouldn't happen today.

He almost didn't see Henderson.

The tall man in the black coat didn't immediately register.

When he saw him closer he remembered.

He'd covered some ground.

Yee pulled the car over.

He would follow on foot.

Henderson leaned over. He was coughing.

Standing still.

Coughing.

The snow was heavy.

Like a blanket coming down.

Yee waited.

Henderson started to walk again, keeping his head down, forcing his steps through the snow.

Yee kept a few paces behind Henderson.

They weren't close to base.

That surprised Yee.

He thought Henderson would have a place closer to the main gate.

Maybe one of the yogwans near the Mustang Club.

Not this far away.

This was Yee's part of town.

Americans here were a rarity.

Yee was curious.

Henderson took a step.

Leaned over and coughed.

Continued the sequence for several steps.

Yee wanted to help, but waited.

He watched Henderson leave the street and go into a yogwan.

A rooming house.

For Koreans.

Never Americans.

Henderson coughed again.

Yee could hear him from the street and walked into the yogwan's courtyard.

Henderson was struggling with the key to his room.

He coughed again.

It was a hideous, violent hack this time. He held his sides and bent over.

While Yee watched, Henderson fell to the ground.

It was the second time Yee had watched him fall.

This time he didn't look like he was going to get up.

The door was about ten yards from Yee.

Running the few steps, Yee's boots making new tracks in the snow.

Henderson's face was gray.

He looked at Yee and said nothing.

Henderson's eyes started to close.

Yee kneeled in the snow.

He needed to get Henderson into the room.

Mr. Yee held out his hand.

"The key?"

The old man's eyes opened. He handed Yee his key and started to cough again.

Yee had to get him into the room. He put Henderson's arm over his own shoulder and hoisted.

The old man was heavy.

Dead weight.

❊ ❊ ❊

Yee felt for a light and found a bulb hanging in the center of the room.

The room was barely warmer than outside. Slamming the door shut with his boot, he struggled with Henderson, pushing and pulling him toward a mat in the corner.

He spread a quilt over Henderson and looked at the stove.

The fire had gone out.

There were three bricks of charcoal next to the stove.

At least he could make a fire.

Henderson's face didn't look any better.

He mouthed a few words.

Scarcely more than whispers.

Yee knew what he needed to do.

An herbalist's shop was two blocks away. Yee would get ingredients and make a tea. It would soothe the old man's throat and stop the cough.

It wouldn't take him long.

Yee told Henderson he would be back.

Henderson started to cough again.

It was a terrible cough. The wracking convulsions were worse than any before.

Yee put his hand on Henderson's chest.

Don't die, he thought.

He needed to hurry.

The street was barely visible now. The snow had come back even stronger than before. Yee arrived at the door to the herbalist's shop. The place was open.

Yee had watched his grandmother make the tea many times. He thought he knew what to get.

The herbalist weighed the ingredients and wrapped them in newspaper.

Yee was glad to help the old man.

He felt grateful to the Americans. He'd worked with them since he was a kid.

He would be glad to help Henderson.

He stepped onto the street and crossed against traffic.

Taking his life in his hands.

Even in good weather, drivers didn't stop for pedestrians.

Yee held the pack of barks and herbs.

The room was silent. Henderson lay on the mat with the quilt covering him.

He was breathing at least.

Yee held Henderson's wrist and felt for a pulse.

It was regular.

Maybe the old man just needed sleep.

That was it.

He just needed sleep.

Again, the coughing.

And then silence.

Henderson looked at Yee.

Yee saw gratitude in the old man's eyes.

He spoke.

"Thanks for your help.

What's your name?"

"My name is Yee."

He busied himself at the electric kettle, putting together the tea. It would do the old man some good, anyway.

Maybe it would stop the cough.

The old man's voice was weak. "You speak good English."

"I work at Camp Long."

"I know," the old man said, "You work with Trinity."

"My boss."

"I have a secret," Henderson said. "I need to talk to him."

Yee held a cup toward the old man.

"Drink this. It's good for you."

"Tell Trinity something for me."

Yee held the tea near Henderson's gray lips.

"What do you want me to tell him?"

Henderson's eye started to close. He didn't speak for a minute.

"Tell Trinity I have something to tell him. It's important. I don't have much time."

"You're leaving soon?"

Henderson would need medical attention.

Yee knew that.

"I'm dying, Yee."

Henderson's brow furrowed.

"I'm terminal."

There was no sentimentality in his voice.

"Tell Trinity I need to see him."

Yee nodded.

SLEEPWALKING

So what was he looking for?

Trinity pushed through the snow.

The sheepskin coat was good. Mr. Kim's men did good work.

Where was he going?

The bartender had said Major Friend was number fucking ten.

Number ten.

The absolute worst.

She might as well have spit when she said it.

Why?

And what did Kilkenny mean saying Friend was dirty?

He needed to talk to Friend.

He didn't look forward to it.

Friend was an asshole.

The MP at the main gate threw a salute when Trinity passed his station.

Friend would be in his office.

Doing nothing.

* * *

The Spec 4 in Friend's office looked at Trinity.

"He's not in," she said.

"You expect him to…"

"I don't expect he'll be here until tomorrow."

Something close to a smile crossed her face.

"Try Mr. Kim at the tailor shop. He left a message for the major."

Trinity thanked her.

There was a short-timer's calendar behind her desk.

He reached for the door and heard her.

"Hey, Mr. Trinity," she said.

He looked back at the desk. There was more than a hint of a smile on the soldier's face.

She was grinning and giving Trinity a fist pump.

* * *

The street was filled with snow. He heard the scrape of a snow-plow blade from the end of the street.

With luck, Mr. Kim would be at his shop.

* * *

The tailor shop was closed.

No Kim.

No Friend.

Trinity regretted letting Yee off.

Yee would have known where Mr. Kim lived.

That would have made things simpler for Trinity.

MR. KIM

Yee started back to the base. If he was lucky, he would be able to flag down a jeep. One of the KATUSA soldiers would give him a ride back. He needed to see Trinity and let him know about Henderson's condition.

The old soldier looked terrible.

Henderson knew his own condition.

He was dying.

Trinity could get Henderson the medical attention he needed.

Fortunately, Yee's wife hadn't been expecting him.

He would still get home at the usual time.

The same time he had come home from Camp Long for close to thirty years. He'd risen from a kid shining GI's boots to an interpretor's job.

Yee was good at his job, and he was proud of the position he held. He was loyal to the Americans who had helped when he

was young. Without the help of those GI's, Yee didn't know what

would have become of him.

He had to pass the Mustang Club on his way to Camp Long.

He could get a ride from there.

If there was no ride, it wasn't a far walk.

He walked through the alleys behind the Mustang Club

quickly.

He didn't like the place. It made him uncomfortable.

Yee saw Mr. Kim. He was going into the club.

Yee didn't trust Kim.

Unlike Yee, Mr. Kim's family was rich.

His parents had paid money to insure Kim's induction as a

KATUSA.

That was how Kim had gotten his start in the black market.

Yee was curious. What business would Mr. Kim have at the

Mustang Club? Korean men didn't usually go there.

Yee followed Kim and stood by the back door. He could see

into the place, but not be seen.

Kim was a fat bully. He was talking to the bartender, giving her a hard time.

They were the only two people in the place.

Kim was pushing his weight around. It sounded like he was making threats.

"You know who did it, don't you?"

The bartender was frightened.

"Which one? The old one?"

Kim slapped her. Yee felt the force of the blow even from a distance.

"You know who did it," Kim said. "Friend. He did it, didn't he?"

She shook her head. "Not Friend."

"Where is she?"

The bartender stared at him. "They took her away."

"Dead?"

"Friend didn't do it," the bartender said. "It was a younger one."

"Give me his name," Kim said.

The bartender shook her head.

"They don't know his name. You ask them. They don't know. They're out there looking right now. Don't worry. They'll find him."

"When they find him, tell them to keep him safe," Kim said. "I can use him."

Kim left.

Yee left in the opposite direction. Back to base.

He needed to talk to Trinity.

THE VILLE

Sundown already.

The days were lengthening, Trinity thought. The tailor's shop was a dead end.

He thought about going back to Friend's office to get a copy of Friend's schedule.

Instead, he got into the Impala and started back to the office.

* * *

With Mr. Yee at home for the rest of the afternoon, Trinity could concentrate on his card-flipping skills and maybe improve them.

The windshield wipers were working overtime. Trinity turned the defroster up full blast and still couldn't see more than a few feet in front of the car.

Then he saw Major Friend.

Friend was sitting in the back seat of his jeep, heading in the opposite direction.

One of the KATUSAs was driving.

Trinity continued slowly into the storm until he felt that it would be safe to follow.

He turned the car around in the parking lot of the base bowling alley.

It wasn't difficult to catch up with the jeep. The driver was going under the base speed limit. Trinity tailed the jeep.

Friend wouldn't turn around.

❋ ❋ ❋

"Going back to the ville?"

The MP on duty at the main gate looked surprised.

"I got some business with Major Friend up there."

Trinity pointed toward the ville.

Friend's jeep was out of sight. Trinity would need to hurry to catch up.

"Hope he doesn't go to fast. I'm supposed to follow him. I don't know where he's going."

"Down by the bus station, I believe sir."

The MP turned around and yelled at the other MP on duty.

"Hey Dave, doesn't Friend have a place... I mean doesn't Major Friend sometimes go to the bus station? Near there?"

The other MP came to the window. "Evening, Mr. Trinity. You're asking about Major Friend?"

Trinity watched the first MP give a look to the second. It was a look of exasperation mixed with caution.

"Right," Trinity said. "Where does he normally go?"

The second MP didn't mind talking about Friend at all.

"Unofficially, sir? I'd say that your chances of finding him in his hootch would be excellent. Right side of the street. Just by the bus station."

Trinity wondered.

Did the use of the word 'unofficially' mean anything in particular, or was it just the cop covering his ass?

The first MP sat down.

The second MP wasn't quite done.

"I'd have to say your chances of finding him there would be excellent on any given day, sir. Tonight might be a particularly good time."

The second MP was jazzed.

Practically beaming.

"Thanks," Trinity said.

"You guys staying warm in there?"

He knew the answer. Between the installed heat and unauthorized space heaters, guard shacks were often the warmest place on base.

The MP nodded.

"You bet," he said. "And have an *outstanding* night."

"Same to you," Trinity said.

"And I hope you catch up with the major really quick."

Trinity returned the MP's salute.

The sun was down , and the twin beams of the Impala's headlights cut through the snow.

* * *

The bus station lay outside the usual GI orbit. Trinity caught up with the jeep near the entrance to one of the bays where a bus had stopped.

Diesel smoke billowed into the snowfall.

The bus station was on the edge of the off-limits area.

It was off-limits for a variety of reasons.

It was too large and too hard for the base to monitor the activities of the soldiers in the area. The town wasn't particularly large, but policy only allowed GI access to areas near the camp.

* * *

The KATUSA driver sat stock-still in the jeep. Friend had to be a bastard.

He'd left the kid in jeep on the coldest night of the year.

Trinity leaned against the driver's door.

"Where did Friend go to?"

The driver, startled, turned toward Trinity.

His nametag read CHUN.

PFC Chun.

Trinity wished Mr. Yee was here.

He could have used a few words with this driver.

Chun smiled and pointed his finger toward a nearby door.

"Major Friend."

Trinity slapped the top of the door.

"Thanks, Chun. Stay warm."

✳ ✳ ✳

Friend was up to something.

Trinity's would find out what that something was.

Kilkenny wasn't an idiot, and neither was the MP at the gate.

The KATUSA driver had been happy to point out Friend's hootch.

Friend looked guilty of something.

He met Trinity at the door of the hootch.

Blocking Trinity from seeing the place.

"What can I do for you, Mr. Trinity?"

Something about the inflection on the word 'mister' irritated Trinity.

He felt like shoving the bastard into the lousy hootch and working him over.

"I need to talk to you, Friend."

Friend was alone. The room behind him was dark.

"I'm afraid that's not convenient right now, Trinity. What's it about?"

Trinity paused.

What the hell *was* it about?

"It's about a Spec 4 Gentle, Major. He's three days short."

Trinity looked back at the street. The KATUSA had turned the lights off in the jeep.

"Spec 4 Gentle... I'm trying to find him."

"Gentle," Friend said. He exhaled. "Yeah. We better talk. Give me a minute and I'll meet you over there."

He pointed up the street from the bus station to a teahouse.

"It won't take long," Trinity said.

"I said, Mr. Trinity, that I would meet you in a few minutes."

Friend shut the door.

❋ ❋ ❋

The smell of fresh doughnuts in the brightly lit teahouse reminded Trinity of home.

He sat in an empty booth with a cup of instant coffee in front of him, waiting for Major Friend.

The place wasn't crowded. Trinity went to the counter and brought back a bag of the doughnuts. The smell of the doughnuts and the marks made by the grease on the bags were promising.

He plunged one of the doughnuts into the instant coffee.

Friend had said he'd meet him in a few minutes.

Trinity looked at his watch.

It had been longer than that.

DARK YOGWAN

Yee knew Trinity wouldn't be at the office.

He went there anyway. As he expected, no Trinity.

Yee looked on his own desk. The same paperwork he'd left and a handwritten note from one of the KATUSA soldiers.

He picked it up and read it. This one wanted to see him.

Could they meet at the KATUSA snack bar?

He put the letter in his shirt pocket, under his quilted vest.

He had only had to wait a couple of minutes before getting a ride from the early shift MPs back up the hill to the camp.

He crossed the street to Trinity's quarters and knocked hard on the door.

No answer.

Trinity would still be in the ville.

Yee needed to tell Trinity about the old man and he needed to tell him about Kim.

Time to find another ride down to the ville.

He waited. This time at the main gate.

He was tired. It had been a hell of a long day and a half and it wasn't over yet.

He decided to grab a cab.

The lights were dark in the yogwan where he left Caleb Henderson.

Henderson still lay under the covers. He hadn't moved since Yee left. Yee put another brick into the charcoal stove, glancing at the window to make sure it was open a crack. The moon was overhead, and the snow had stopped for the moment.

Trinity needed know about this. Henderson was a war hero. Trinity would want to know.

Henderson said he was dying, but he hadn't said how fast. He was sleeping now. A shallow breathing from his nose.

Yee started to make a tea.

There were customs that needed to be observed when a person was dying. Henderson didn't have any family now. He said his son was missing. It was sad for a man to leave the world alone.

Yee looked at the old man. Would Henderson die tonight?

It wasn't impossible. Some people knew when they were about to die.

If this was Henderson's night, Yee couldn't leave him. That would be unthinkable.

The water came to a boil, and Yee measured in the ingredients he'd bought at the herbalist's shop.

Steam rose from the kettle. It would be tough getting Henderson to drink the tea.

Yee poured two cups and sipped one of them.

Where was Trinity?

Trinity didn't know where Yee was.

There was no use wondering why Trinity hadn't shown up.

Trinity wouldn't come here.

Yee would have to take a chance.

He didn't like leaving Henderson, but he had to find Trinity.

The scene at the bar also bothered Yee. What was going on between Kim and the bartender? Why did he slap her?

Who was the woman they mentioned?

There were too many questions.

Yee was afraid that his mental disharmony would affect Henderson.

He tried to calm his mind and was almost successful.

Henderson awoke.

CAFE LIGHTS

More Korean music in the teahouse.

Trinity was still waiting for Major Friend.

To Trinity, the song sounded like a soundtrack for a strangling.

He ordered another cup of coffee and stared at the door of the café.

Friend wouldn't just take off, would he?

Trinity watched a bus diesel out of the station. Without stops, it would be in Seoul well before midnight.

❈ ❈ ❈

Friend, smelling like booze and after-shave, sat down across from Trinity.

He shook off the waitress.

"What do you know about this soldier?"

"Gentle?"

Trinity tried to focus on Friend. The lights of the café were bright. Every crevice and pore in the major's face was exposed.

"Exactly," Friend said. "I'm afraid I've had some disturbing news about him. I may need to have you pick him up before the Korean authorities."

Friend had more than one drink in the last twenty minutes.

Trinity was sure of that.

The precise slur of the officer's voice was as telling as a field sobriety test.

He would let Friend talk.

Friend had no authority over Trinity.

Both men knew it.

Trinity leaned forward in his seat.

The day was beginning to feel endless. The café lights added to the hallucinatory effect.

"What did you hear?"

Friend pursed his lips. "Apparently there has been a death." He stopped. Looked briefly at the ceiling. "A murder. I just heard about it. Of course, I would have told you about it. As soon as I could get to my office."

"Who told you about this?"

"The Korean..." Friend stopped. Hesitated. "I'm sure you know Mr. Kim. Everyone knows him."

"Mr. Kim who makes suits?"

Friend nodded.

Kim was his source?

"Who died?"

"A waitress from the Mustang Club. Unfortunately, it seems certain that our young soldier was involved."

Trinity stood up and pulled on his coat.

"Does Kim know where Gentle is?"

"If he had, I would have gone there myself, Trinity."

Friend's suggestion didn't sound likely.

How long had the bastard kept Trinity waiting?

Twenty minutes at least. Possibly a half an hour. Then he

shows up after downing a couple of quick shots and slapping on some Aqua-Velva.

"You couldn't have told me this earlier?" Trinity pointed in the direction of Friend's hootch.

"I wasn't…" Friend hesitated. "I needed to be sure of jurisdiction. Obviously the provost…"

"We're wasting time, Major."

Friend stared at Trinity. "I beg your pardon?"

"You heard me. When were you planning to tell me about this? After the locals lock our guy up?"

"I'm sure they won't…"

"You can't be sure of that, Major. We need to find Gentle before they do.

"You're out of line, Trinity. Way out of line."

Trinity ignored him.

"Did you see him last night?"

"When? Last night? Of course not."

"Then the first you heard of his absence was from Mr. Kim?"

"Not exactly," Friend said. "I heard from Sergeant Kilkenny that he didn't make formation. Naturally I was concerned. Particularly since he only has a few days left in country."

Friend's smile was not convincing.

He's not even a good liar, Trinity thought. Kilkenny hadn't told Friend anything.

"So you told Kilkenny to write Gentle up?"

Friend furrowed his brow. "Well, under the circumstances, I felt that... non-judicial punishment would probably be in order."

Without hearing any facts, Friend had decided what he would do.

The hook wasn't set. Trinity decided to let out the line.

He stood up and put on the Stetson.

"I guess that's all I need to know."

Friend looked smug.

The liquor had done wonders for his temperament.

He extended his hand.

Gave Trinity a hearty I'm-not-holding-any-grudges grip.

"Let me know if you see Gentle. I just might have to pull some strings."

"He's supposed to leave in two days, Major."

"I'm aware of that." Friend dropped his hand. "And he's only one of many soldiers on this base who look to me for discipline and order."

It was difficult for Trinity to imagine a worse example of military leadership.

Trinity had to find Gentle

MEDICINAL TEA

Caleb Henderson awakened in the small yogwan. The charcoal heater glowed in the center of the yellow linoleum floor.

He felt groggy.

Maybe fumes from the charcoal?

He was barely aware of his surroundings. He vaguely remembered giving his room away, but now he was in another practically identical room.

The Korean man squatting on the floor near him.

Who was he?

He looked familiar.

Had he seen him before?

He tried raising his head.

No luck.

Turned his head toward the man instead.

"Who are you, again?"

"My name is Yee. I work with Trinity."

That helped.

Henderson remembered talking to Trinity.

Had it been yesterday? The day before yesterday? He couldn't remember. For some reason, he needed to see Trinity.

"Yee," he said. "Is Trinity here?"

Yee shook his head no.

"I need to see him."

"Do you need to go to the doctor?"

"Doctor's can't help," Henderson said.

"I've made some tea. You should have some."

The last day had been a blur.

Things had been blurry for a number of years. What had happened to his son? Why couldn't he remember? When he thought he was getting close to the truth, the gray wall of obscurity rose in front of him and blocked his view.

It didn't matter how long he walked around the base.

He could do it for another fifteen or twenty years and he knew he wouldn't come any closer to the truth.

He knew he didn't have fifteen or twenty years.

The end was near for him.

Why had he told Trinity about his son? He had never dropped his defenses before.

He had never admitted he didn't know what happened to his son.

It would be closer to the truth to say he couldn't remember what happened.

In a way, the truth felt worse.

He slept for what seemed like a moment and awakened again. Yee was still there.

"I'd like to see Trinity," Henderson said.

"I'll try to get him," Yee said, but he didn't move.

POUND OF FLESH

Who the hell did Trinity think he was?

Major Stanley Friend stood in the darkness of his office. The woman hadn't been at the hootch of course. She wouldn't cause any more problems.

What did Trinity think?

Trinity didn't know who he was dealing with.

Kim would fulfill his part of the bargain.

Kim's word was good.

But there was a price to be paid.

Kim would extract his pound of flesh.

Unless Friend complied.

Friend pulled the key out of his pocket. It was the correct key.

It would open the arms room.

Briefly, of course. Kim had assured him the key would be returned.

Only a few weapons would be taken. An insignificant number,

really.

And the shortage wouldn't be discovered for months.

There would be an NCO to take the blame.

He thought about the Spec 4 in his office.

They could pin it on her.

She would be perfect.

Friend wouldn't be here then.

It would be the next guy's problem.

The phone rang.

Friend hesitated, and then picked it up.

Kim's voice was ice cool over the phone.

"Major Friend? We need to talk about the woman."

Friend knew he should hang up. Anyone could listen in on this line.

"Listen, Kim..."

Kim interrupted him. "This raises the stakes, Friend."

Friend hung up.

Pulled open the side door of his desk and picked up the Colt.

Slid out the clip. It was loaded.

Holstered the automatic and covered it with his field jacket.

He stood up and walked to the door.

He would find Gentle and take care of him.

LAST REQUEST

It was dark when Trinity saw Mr. Yee.

Of course the snow was still coming down. For the second night in a row the streets were nearly silent.

The weather kept people inside.

Trinity was driving the Impala.

Looking for Gentle.

Back to the Mustang Club?

It made of sense. Wouldn't they know where Gentle had gone?

According to the DJ, the bartender had known Gentle was asleep on the floor.

Who could say if the story Kim told Friend was accurate?

Who was the woman allegedly murdered in the club and why was there no report on his desk?

Why hadn't the provost told him?

Was there even such a woman?

Trinity saw Mr.Yee.

The interpreter had his head down against the snow and wore no hat.

He had on the green quilted jacket he always wore.

Trinity pulled to the side of the street.

Mr. Yee got into the Impala.

His crew cut was covered with snow.

"I found Henderson, Trinity. He's pretty bad off."

"How bad is that?"

Trinity eased the car back onto the empty street.

The street lights looked like halos in the snow.

"More than sick," Mr. Yee said. "He's dying, Trinity. He wants to see you."

"Did you get in touch with the infirmary?"

Mr. Yee shook his head.

"He won't go. Whatever it is he's got, he's had for a while."

"You know his story, don't you?"

Yee looked grim. "Sure, everybody knows about Cal Henderson."

Trinity took a second to let the information sink in. He knew he would have to go see the old man. It was the right thing to do. A last request for an old soldier.

He told Mr. Yee about his conversation with Friend.

"Friend thinks Gentle killed her."

"A this is a girl from the Mustang Club?"

"Apparently."

Mr. Yee didn't look surprised.

"You going to see Henderson?"

"Where is he?"

Yee half turned in his seat and pointed.

"A little yogwan. That's where I left him."

"You sure he won't see the doc?"

"He wants to see you. Could be about his son."

"Show me where."

"What about Gentle?"

Trinity turned to Yee.

"We'll find him."

OVERHEAD SPEAKER

They stood together, hand in hand now, in front of the bus terminal.

The last bus to Seoul left later that night.

She would take a cab to the airport and wait for a flight back to the states.

Gentle wanted to say something.

Something reasonable.

He didn't like the idea of letting her go.

What had this day meant to her?

Wandering around for a day in Korea with a GI she barely knew.

He thought about the little shop near the yogwan. She had admired the beautiful silk robes in the window.

He should have bought one for her.

They had a brief conversation about meeting later.

No specifics.

He had her address.

She had his.

Gentle knew the score.

So long, been nice to know you.

Why would it be any different?

They had eaten lunch together and then disappeared into a movie theater where they spent an afternoon watching a martial arts movie and then a romantic drama of some kind.

They had kissed in the theater.

Shyly at first and then with more abandon.

Then it had been time to go to the bus station.

The bus station down the street from the yogwan where they had met.

Where she had let him share her room.

She looked at him.

The bus would be leaving soon.

Her eyes were extraordinarily blue.

"I'd like to see you again," she said.

He put his hands on her waist and felt her move closer to him.

The overhead speaker announced the departure of another bus.

Not her bus.

Gentle and Harmony were in a different world.

"I'll be going back now," he said.

"To the base?"

"What can they do to me? I'm leaving the day after tomorrow."

"I could go with you," she said.

Just like that, the world changed.

Gentle looked at Harmony.

She was looking at him. Searching his face. Was she in doubt of his answer?

He kissed her.

A bus left the terminal.

A trail of diesel smoke following.

People walked around Gentle and Harmony, who stood forever on the concrete floor.

She pulled away slightly and whispered. "I'll stay with you until you go."

"You'll need a place."

They both knew where the yogwan was.

It was still early in the evening. The innkeeper had a room. He pointed toward a different room with a sliding door.

Yellow linoleum and charcoal stove in the middle of the room.

Gentle put her backpack down inside the door.

She had let him carry it.

He turned to her and their kiss lasted even longer than the one in the terminal.

❊ ❊ ❊

They were hungry. She looked for the salami and found it in her backpack.

"Damn," she said.

"What's wrong?"

"Nothing, really."

She rummaged through the pack.

"My knife. I can't find it."

He remembered her Swiss Army knife.

He stood up.

"We need more food anyway. I'll get a knife while I'm out."

She kept looking through the bag.

"It must have dropped out of my bag."

He kissed her again.

"I'll be back soon," he said.

WEAK BUT STILL ALIVE

Henderson was delirious.

Trinity slid the door of the room back into place and turned the light on.

The old man lay on the mattress, talking.

Trinity had walked into a private conversation.

A one sided conversation held in the past and the present.

"He's gone now. That's the only thing I'm sure of."

Henderson's words were short and breathless.

Labored.

"Drowned. My fault."

Trinity turned toward Mr. Yee.

"Any of this sound familiar?"

Yee shook his head.

"He only told me he wanted to talk to you."

❊ ❊ ❊

Trinity knelt beside the old man's bed.

Took Henderson's wrist.

Felt the pulse.

Weak, but still alive.

Trinity looked up. Fished in his pocket and flipped his car keys to Mr. Yee.

"Take the Impala. We need to get him a doctor."

Mr. Yee left.

❊ ❊ ❊

Henderson turned to Trinity.

"Before the doctor," he said. "I need to talk to you first."

"I'm right here," Trinity said.

"You're a priest?"

Henderson's eyes searched the corner of the room behind Trinity's head.

"No."

Henderson squinted.

The effort of conversation made him tired.

"It's been a long time since I confessed," Henderson said.

How long would it take for Yee to get a medic down here?

It would probably be too late.

Too late for a chaplain, too.

Henderson opened his mouth then closed it.

"My son's out there."

Trinity patted the old man's hand.

Go ahead, he thought.

"My son…" Henderson said.

"What happened with your son?"

Henderson was startled.

He stared at Trinity.

"Saving a little boy. He drowned."

"Here?"

"The river outside camp. I remember now."

"How long have you been coming here?"

"I don't know," Henderson said. "I think I've been here several times."

"So your son was a hero. Like you."

"*He* was a hero. You can draw your own conclusions about me."

Henderson's face was more pale than Trinity had seen it.

Where was Yee?

Could they get some medical help?

Would it make any difference?

"You're a hero, too," Trinity said. "You're Caleb Henderson."

Henderson's eyes flickered.

"That was a long time ago. That's why I wanted to see you."

The confession.

Trinity leaned closer. Put his ear closer to Henderson's mouth.

"I can hear you."

Henderson moaned.

It was a moan, less of pain than world weariness.

The exhalation at the end of a race.

Trinity was Henderson's only witness. The old man wouldn't last much longer.

"Tell me what you need to say," Trinity said. "Better now, before the others get here."

There wouldn't be any others.

Yee might get an ambulance, but it would only be able to take the old man's body back.

"My son didn't want to serve. I told him no son of mine would run away from duty.

So that was it?

"He wasn't a fighter. He should never have served. At least I pulled *some* strings..."

"Strings?"

"Kept him from Nam."

"So he was stationed here?"

"This is where he died. I don't remember everything, and some things I try to forget."

Henderson closed his eyes.

Trinity felt for a pulse.

Checked the carotid artery.

Checked for a heartbeat.

Still alive.

* * *

Mr. Yee stood by the door.

Trinity looked back at him. "How long have you been there?"

"A little while, boss. They're sending an ambulance down."

Trinity walked over to Mr. Yee.

Whispered.

"Did you know about this?"

"The part about the river? It's pretty well known. The son drowned. Didn't he save a kid? That's always been the story."

Trinity nodded.

"I've got to go now," Yee said. "I got to meet with somebody."

Trinity nodded again.

Henderson could barely speak. "You're a priest, aren't you?"

"I'll get one for you," Trinity said.

Henderson slightly shook his head. "There won't be time."

Trinity sat by the old man's side, listening.

Some of Henderson's words were incoherent, but enough were not.

Trinity listened.

A REMARKABLE WEAPON

The heft of the .45 always surprised Friend.

Truly a remarkable weapon, he thought.

He wondered if he would need to use it.

He covered the holstered .45 with his field jacket. He needed to take care of Gentle. Gentle had seen him. Gentle could implicate him.

Friend went outside to the waiting jeep.

Where the hell was PFC Chun?

To hell with him, Friend thought.

He started the jeep.

✻ ✻ ✻

The MP's saluted Friend as he passed the gate.

✻ ✻ ✻

Friend watched Gentle give the blonde girl a kiss outside the yogwan.

Friend's eyes narrowed with suspicion and anger.

He'd seen her before.

Last night.

How the hell had they ended up together? And so near his place?

Nobody was supposed to know about this place.

Kim.

It had to be that bastard.

The whole thing was a setup.

He'd been set up.

Set up by Kim.

Before everything happened.

The blonde must be in on it too, he thought.

He watched Gentle walk down the street.

He felt the .45 with his left hand.

Tempted to take care of things at once, he restrained himself.

He had a better plan.

Gentle might regret leaving her.

THE SILK ROBE

The woman in the store let Gentle in.

She smiled.

Gentle thought about Harmony.

He wanted to stay with her.

He pointed to the window and the silk robe. The woman took it from the display and placed it on the counter.

Harmony would like it.

"You can wrap it for me?"

Gentle used hand signals to illustrate his question.

She smoothed the robe and placed it in a box.

Held it up for his inspection.

Gentle nodded.

KATUSA SNACK BAR

After talking to the medics, Yee drove to the KATUSA snack bar.

No matter what the KATUSA had to say, Yee had to make it quick.

PFC Chun sat at the first table.

The place was deserted. Yee recognized PFC Chun. He thought he would, when he read the note.

Major Friend's driver.

"You needed to talk?"

PFC Chun signaled Yee to sit down.

"Major Friend," he said.

"Your boss? You're his driver?"

PFC Chun nodded.

"I need to tell you something about him."

❉ ❉ ❉

Yee stood up.

"You did the right thing, Chun."

He shook the KATUSA's hand.

PFC Chun looked relieved. It couldn't have been easy to tell Yee these things.

There wasn't any time to spare.

He needed Trinity.

Yee's authority didn't extend to arrests.

Friend could be dangerous.

Not *could*, he thought.

Friend *would* be dangerous.

❋ ❋ ❋

Yee got back into the Impala.

Hoping he wouldn't be too late.

LOVER-BOY

Harmony opened the door.

Whoever was knocking wasn't going to stop.

She looked at the man outside the door. She'd seen him before. He was the man who had brushed by her last night. He'd been in such a hurry.

She recognized the mustache.

"Who are you?" she said.

He pulled the .45 from his holster and forced his way into the room.

Shut the door.

Held the automatic loosely at his side.

"You know Gentle?"

"What are you talking about?"

She couldn't help herself. The words came out gasping.

Friend ignored her.

"Do you know him?"

"What do you want?"

He motioned for her to sit down on the floor.

"I want you to shut up. We're just going to wait here for lover-boy."

She felt her breath grow shallow.

"No."

Friend shook his head.

"He's coming with me."

He pointed the .45 at the door.

"Dead or alive."

"You can't," she said.

He turned toward her.

Dropped the gun to his side.

"You don't expect him soon, do you?"

"I don't…"

Harmony stopped herself.

"He'll be back any minute."

Friend smiled.

"Sorry, I don't believe you."

He walked toward her.

"I've got an idea," he said.

Closer.

"Why don't you and I get better acquainted?"

BLACK STILETTO

A hardware stall made from plywood and canvas stood at the end of the block.

Gentle walked back toward the yogwan.

Harmony would like the robe. She'd practically picked it out herself.

Passing the stall, Gentle remembered the knife. He could find one here.

The man in the stall pulled the long black stiletto from beneath the glass and showed it to Gentle.

Gentle pulled out a fistful of won notes.

He wouldn't need Korean money back in the world.

Would he be able to go with Harmony?

Probably not.

But they would meet soon.

They'd talked about San Francisco.

RELAX

Mr. Yee slammed on the brakes. Trinity turned to him.

"You're sure this is the place?"

"That's what Chun told me."

The door was open and Trinity and Yee raced into the building.

From the hallway, Trinity heard the sound of a male, American voice.

"Relax," the man said.

Trinity recognized the voice.

Friend.

Trinity measured the distance and smashed the thin door with his boot.

Friend turned away from Harmony.

He lunged for the .45.

Not quickly enough.

Mr. Yee reached the gun before him and hammered the barrel

down on Friend's head.

The major crumpled.

Trinity pulled out handcuffs and slapped them on Friend's wrists.

He heard Mr. Yee yell.

"Look out, Trinity..."

Trinity turned around to see Spec 4 Gentle.

Charging in to the room, holding the switchblade in front of himself.

"No Ben," Harmony screamed.

Gentle dropped the knife.

THE ZIPPO

Death arrived for Caleb Henderson as gently as snow on a dark night.

Gentle and Harmony sat with the chaplain at Henderson's bedside in the base infirmary.

Trinity stood in the doorway.

Harmony had already thanked Henderson for giving her his room that night.

Henderson was holding her hand when he died.

❊ ❊ ❊

"One more favor?" Gentle said.

"What do you need?"

Trinity looked in the rear view mirror of the Impala at the couple.

He would take them to the airport and make sure they left

safely.

He'd pulled strings to get them on the same flight.

Gentle dug in his pocket.

Pulled out a Zippo lighter.

"This belongs to the DJ at the Mustang Club. Could you get it back to him?"

Trinity reached over the back seat and took the lighter.

It was engraved with a series of indentations.

Braille.

"Sure," he said.

"Thanks."

Gentle settled back in his seat.

Trinity looked in the rear-view mirror again.

They were on their way home.

THE STARS AND STRIPES

The bartender gave Yee directions to the DJ's house.

She told Yee she didn't expect the DJ would come back to work.

He lived a long way from the bar.

✾ ✾ ✾

Trinity and Mr. Yee pulled up to the DJ's house.

The woman answering the door must have been the DJ's mother.

She smiled at the two men and spoke quickly to Yee.

"She says he's almost done with his lessons. We're welcome to wait."

Trinity and Yee sat in the front room of the apartment.

It was similar to other places Trinity had seen with yellow linoleum, charcoal heater, a calendar on the wall.

Three children came out of the back room.

Black and white school uniforms for both the boy and the two girls.

Blind children.

They chatted on their way out.

The DJ came out of the back room and Yee spoke to him.

The DJ smiled, spoke to Yee, and held out his hand.

"He missed the lighter," Yee said. "It has a special meaning for him. He is very grateful."

Trinity shook the DJ's hand then handed him the lighter. "You're welcome."

Yee turned to Trinity.

"The mother says that he teaches English to lots of kids. Some of them have American fathers. He's doing work not everyone would do."

Trinity looked at the DJ.

The young man looked more at ease than he had the other night.

He shook the DJ's hand again and started to leave.

At the door, he paused and glanced at a small, framed *Stars and Stripes* article.

Yellow from age.

The headline's date was over twenty years old:

HERO'S SON DIES IN RIVER RESCUING BLIND BOY.

The two men walked out of the house and onto the street.

New snow was falling.

Made in the USA
San Bernardino, CA
27 January 2020